Savannah Spectator

Blind Item

The *Savannah Spectator* presents its very own production of the tragic love story *Romeo and Juliet!*

The Scene: Two rivals, both vying for the same senatorial seat.

The Lovers: The cool, beautiful daughter just returned from abroad to support her father's campaign, and the dashing yet cerebral son of Savannah's first family, whose "honest" father has been visited by scandal.

Act I: Romeo meets Juliet at a Montague function and passionate sparks fly. But what is a Capulet doing there?

Act II: A secret tryst at the beach and another at a historic inn. Lots of sex, but so far, no sympathetic priest or nurse to help our lovers.

Can these two star-crossed lovers survive their fathers' bitter rivalry? Will Juliet's ardor be extinguished when her father discovers his only daughter has been parking her glass slippers under a Montague bed? A rose by any other name would smell just as sweet, but a scandalous affair between the names involved here is the sweetest smelling of all! You can bet this reporter will be sitting on the edge of her seat for Act III to begin!

D1044413

Dear Reader,

Welcome to another fabulous month at Silhouette Desire, where we offer you the best in passionate, powerful and provocative love stories. You'll want to delve right in to our latest DYNASTIES: THE DANFORTHS title with Anne Marie Winston's highly dramatic *The Enemy's Daughter*— you'll never guess who the latest Danforth bachelor has gotten involved with! And the steam continues to rise when Annette Broadrick returns to the Desire line with a brand-new series, THE CRENSHAWS OF TEXAS. These four handsome brothers will leave you breathless, right from the first title, *Branded*.

Read a Silhouette Desire novel from *his* point of view in our new promotion MANTALK. Eileen Wilks continues this series with her highly innovative and intensely emotional story *Meeting at Midnight*. Kristi Gold continues her series THE ROYAL WAGER with another confirmed bachelor about to meet his match in *Unmasking the Maverick Prince*. How comfortable can *A Bed of Sand* be? Well, honey, if you're lying on it with the hero of Laura Wright's latest novel…who cares! And the always enjoyable Roxanne St. Claire, whom *Publishers Weekly* calls "an author who's on the fast track to making her name a household one," is scorching up the pages with *The Fire Still Burns*.

Happy reading,

Melissa Jeglinski

Melissa Jeglinski
Senior Editor, Silhouette Desire

Please address questions and book requests to:
Silhouette Reader Service
U.S.: 3010 Walden Ave., P.O. Box 1325, Buffalo, NY 14269
Canadian: P.O. Box 609, Fort Erie, Ont. L2A 5X3

THE ENEMY'S DAUGHTER
ANNE MARIE WINSTON

Silhouette® Desire

Published by Silhouette Books

America's Publisher of Contemporary Romance

Special thanks and acknowledgment are given to
Anne Marie Winston for her contribution
to the DYNASTIES: THE DANFORTHS series.

For Laurie
It's good to see you glow,
And for Bert
Welcome to the tribe!

 SILHOUETTE BOOKS

ISBN 0-373-76603-3

THE ENEMY'S DAUGHTER

Visit Silhouette Books at www.eHarlequin.com

Printed in U.S.A.

ANNE MARIE WINSTON

RITA® Award finalist and bestselling author Anne Marie Winston loves babies she can give back when they cry, animals in all shapes and sizes and just about anything that blooms. When she's not writing, she's managing a house full of animals and teenagers, reading anything she can find and trying *not* to eat chocolate. She will dance at the slightest provocation and weeds her gardens when she can't see the sun for the weeds anymore. You can learn more about Anne Marie's novels by visiting her Web site at www.annemariewinston.com.

DYNASTIES: THE DANFORTHS

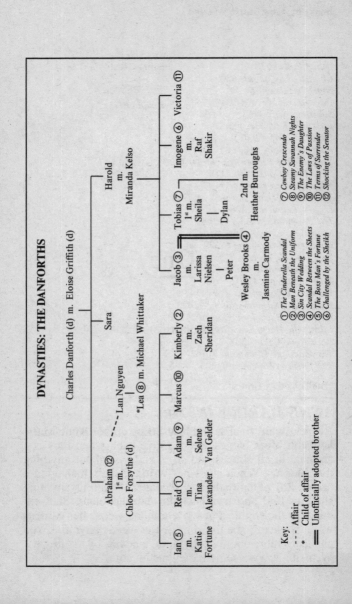

Charles Danforth (d) m. Eloise Griffith (d)

Sara

Harold
m.
Miranda Kelso

Abraham ⑫
1st m.
Chloe Forsythe (d)

Lan Nguyen

*Lea ⑧ m. Michael Whittaker

Ian ⑤
m.
Katie
Fortune

Reid ①
m.
Tina
Alexander

Kimberly ②
m.
Zach
Sheridan

Marcus ⑩

Adam ⑨
m.
Selene
Van Gelder

Jacob ③
m.
Larissa
Nielsen
|
Peter

Wesley Brooks ④
m.
Jasmine Carmody

Tobias ⑦
1st m.
Sheila
|
Dylan

2nd m.
Heather Burroughs

Imogene ⑥
m.
Raf
Shakir

Victoria ⑪

Key:
- - - Affair
* Child of affair
═══ Unofficially adopted brother

① *The Cinderella Scandal*
② *Man Beneath the Uniform*
③ *Sin City Wedding*
④ *Scandal Between the Sheets*
⑤ *The Boss Man's Fortune*
⑥ *Challenged by the Sheikh*
⑦ *Cowboy Crescendo*
⑧ *Steamy Savannah Nights*
⑨ *The Enemy's Daughter*
⑩ *The Laws of Passion*
⑪ *Terms of Surrender*
⑫ *Shocking the Senator*

One

The coffee shop was surprisingly busy for the middle of a Wednesday afternoon.

Selene Van Gelder paused just inside the door of D&D's, an upscale coffeehouse located on a bluff above the river's edge in the historic district of Savannah, Georgia. The air conditioning felt wonderful, since the heat was still oppressive in early September. She took several deep breaths, feeling the jittery unease in her stomach increase. This was foolhardy. She shouldn't be here.

She had told herself she needed to go shopping today, but when she'd found herself standing outside the wood-and-brass doors of D&D's with their frosted window panes, it was time to admit to herself that after two months she finally couldn't resist the urge to find out more about Adam Danforth.

So this was his business. At least, partly his, she thought, recalling that he'd said his cousin and his oldest brother were his partners. Breathing deeply of the rich blend of coffee aromas, she looked curiously around the interior.

It was as elegant as she'd expected, but the atmosphere was one of warmth and invitation. Rich dark-paneled wood set off gleaming brass, and café curtains spanned the wide windows on which the Danforth & Co.'s stylized logo, intertwined *D*'s with a lavish ampersand, appeared in gilt letters. Along one wall was an enormous fireplace, though she wondered how often they actually got to use the thing, with a climate as mild as Savannah's.

Strangely, the sight of the fireplace calmed her nerves. It reminded her of her youth growing up in European boarding schools. Roaring fires were more a necessity than a luxury during the chilly northern winters on the Continent. And though one didn't normally think of boarding school as a great place to be, for Selene school had meant comfort and security.

But you're not in Europe anymore, Selene, she reminded herself. No, she was home—if she could really call Savannah home. She supposed it was as familiar as any other place stateside, and at least she had some connection to Savannah, however tenuous it felt. She'd been born here in the heat of a summer evening. And her mother's grave was here, beneath the live oaks in one of the stately old cemeteries where the city's first families routinely were interred.

Her mother. She sighed, wishing she'd known the woman who had given her life. But Elisabetta Horne

Van Gelder had died mere hours after the birth of her only child, breathing just long enough to give Selene her name and bid farewell to the husband who had loved her so dearly. How different, she wondered, might her life be today had her mother lived?

Pulling herself from introspection that she knew from experience would prove painful, she crossed to the counter and ordered a tall cup of D&D's special Brazilian mocha blend to go. She looked around the room at the waiters and the staff working the sophisticated machinery, but she didn't see Adam.

A wave of disappointment swept through her, and she told herself not to be ridiculous. The co-owner of the business, particularly an entrepreneur as wealthy and successful as Adam Danforth was reported to be, would hardly be working behind the counter.

Besides, the last thing either of them needed was a public meeting that could be witnessed by someone who might identify them. Wouldn't that make a nice tidbit for the gossip columns?

It was time to go. She was half regretting the impulse that had brought her here. Hadn't she been telling herself since July that she couldn't get involved with Adam?

Not to mention that it was terribly arrogant of her to assume he would still be interested if she did look him up. After all, she hadn't heard a word from him since she'd received a lovely bouquet of roses and lilies the morning after the dinner-dance where they'd met.

As she turned with her drink in hand, she nearly bumped into a blonde in a trim navy suit behind her. With a quick sidestep, she murmured, "Sorry."

The other woman barely acknowledged her. "Honey," she was saying to her companion, a brunette who looked to be a member of the downtown business community as well, "he is the most gorgeous hunk of man I've seen in ages. Think Josh Hartnett mixed with a healthy dose of a young Tom Cruise. Except Adam's six feet tall." She sighed. "I'd like a piece of that action."

Adam? Selene's attention sharpened, even though she felt as if every person in the place suddenly knew she was eavesdropping.

"Maybe—until he opens his mouth," her friend said. "I won't argue with the hunk definition, but the man is a dead bore. I went out with him once, years ago, and I am tellin' you, my eyes positively glazed over after the first twenty minutes."

The first woman shrugged. "I don't need them to be real bright," she said with a sly laugh.

"That might be the problem." The brunette who'd gone out with the man in question dug her wallet out of her purse. "He's *too* smart. Once he gets rollin' on the ghosts and legends stuff, you might as well order another drink and get out your earplugs. Every time you think he's windin' down he heads off in a new direction."

Selene could barely contain her amusement. The pair *had* to be talking about her Adam.

No! Not your Adam!

Adam Danforth. She supposed that to many women, his fascination with history and local legends might be a trifle boring, but to someone who'd actu-ally enjoyed her university years studying dead languages and ancient literature, he couldn't have been more interesting.

She threaded her way past the other waiting customers toward the door. It was a good thing she hadn't seen him. This had been a stupid move and she would have regretted it had they met again.

Of course she would have.

She had to wait for a large party to enter just as she reached the door, and while she did so, her attention was caught by the spacious bulletin board on the nearest wall. One message read: "SWF seeks SWM to share frangelica cappuccino and opera. Must love small, yappy dogs." There was a phone number beneath. Another was a boldly drawn heart: "Elena, will you marry me?" She smiled and kept reading, even though the entryway had cleared. Apparently this message board had become something of a dating service!

She read another couple of messages, including one extended exchange that the couple involved apparently added to each day. And then she saw it.

To S., my flower garden ghost: I'm wilting without you. Call me. A.

Her breath caught, her heart stuttered. Flower garden ghost? Who else could have written that? And who else could it have been intended for?

Adam. Adam had written that. For her, Selene. Only him. Only her.

Her hands were shaking as she pulled a pen and a notepad from her purse. Without giving herself time to think of the wisdom of what she was doing, she unpinned the small piece of paper and placed it in her pocket. Then she wrote on the notepad.

To A. from your flower garden ghost: The lovely flowers you sent have wilted, too. My thoughts of you haven't. Shall we meet? S.

Quickly, she pinned up her response, then fled the coffeehouse before common sense could prevail. She was halfway down the block before she realized her cell phone was ringing.

Digging it from her pocketbook, she flipped it open. "Hello?"

"Selene!" The voice was rich, husky and deeply accented by the speaker's native French tongue. "How are you, *ma petite*? I am very angry that you have not called to ask me all about the wedding plans."

"Guillemette!" Joy rushed through her. Her boarding school roommate and dearest friend in the world was the daughter of a French family of noble lineage. Willi had recently become engaged to a distant cousin of the queen of England. "How are you?"

"Glowing, dear girl. I want to hear about *you*."

Selene realized she was shrugging. "There's nothing to tell. Life in the States is staid and dull. My father's campaign is chugging along, but I'm staying well out of it. I have no desire to become fodder for the American press."

"What? No handsome men? Shame on them all."

Selene hesitated as Adam's lean features leaped instantly into her head.

"Selene! There *is* a man, isn't there? You can't fool me! I'm the closest thing you have to a sister, and I can read you like a spread book, darling. Now spill."

"That's *open book*, Willi. Get your similes straight."
Ahead of her, there was an empty bench in a small park
just off the street. Heading for it, she spoke again. "It's
not exactly a relationship."

"Start from the beginning," her friend demanded. "I
want to hear everything."

She thought for a moment. "The beginning? Well,
that was actually back in July, about five days after I arrived in Savannah. Do you remember I came home at
Father's request…?"

*"Try to look more cheerful, Selene. If you go to this
fund-raiser looking like that, people are going to notice
you, I can guarantee it." John Van Gelder's voice was
filled with censure.*

*"I don't want to go, Father. It would be one thing to
attend a function to support your senate campaign, but
this is nothing more than spying on Abraham Danforth.
I'm terrible at things like this. Someone is going to find
out." Selene concentrated on shaking out the folds of her
white silk evening gown, avoiding his eyes. Maybe he'd
relent.*

*But her father brushed aside her concern. As he'd
brushed her aside her entire life. "No one will find out
if you don't call attention to yourself. And how would
they know you? You've been out of the country for years.
I don't even know when the last public photo of you was
taken."*

*She did. She'd been nine, home for a visit with her
father in America. Overwhelmed and missing the familiar environs of the exclusive Swiss school where she*

lived, largely ignored by her surviving parent, she'd been crying when the picture was snapped.

Her father's voice cut through the memory. "And it's not spying. All I want you to do is keep your ears open for anything I should know about the Danforth campaign. Danforth can't possibly be as squeaky clean as he appears."

"He isn't," she pointed out. "But he's honest about his mistakes—"

"Right." Her father sneered. "Everyone knows he was forced to welcome that illegitimate Vietnamese daughter into the family, but he managed to turn it into political gold. And before you came home there was an enormous brouhaha when his nanny's kid's body was found right there on his estate. That one almost sank him, but the authorities swear he had nothing to do with it." He snorted. "I wish I had his spin doctors."

Selene sighed. Her arguments fell on deaf ears and in moments she found herself bundled into a car, headed for the Danforth political fund-raiser. Fine, she thought rebelliously. You can make me attend, Father, but you can't make me spy for you.

The dinner-dance was held at the historic Twin Oaks Hotel in downtown Savannah. Selene entered just behind a group of other guests and quickly took stock of the room. Lovely French doors opened onto extensive gardens at the rear of the hotel, while dancers created graceful patterns on the polished wooden dance floor. Other guests mingled around the tables throughout the room.

She quietly headed toward the doors at the back of the room. It would be hot outside, but that was good. No one else was crazy enough to come out in the humid evening air; she could stay ten minutes and then leave.

So there, Father. I've attended the fund-raiser, and gee, so sorry, I didn't hear anything.

As she moved around the edge of the room, she passed the ladies' room and decided to freshen up. When she entered the lounge area, she found a young teenage girl crying there. Selene and another young woman each attempted to comfort her. The child appeared to be having parent troubles, and her distress tore at Selene's all-too-sympathetic heart. Selene knew, however, that she couldn't afford to get involved in the young stranger's problems. After all, she wasn't even on the guest list and she doubted anyone would be thrilled to find a Van Gelder at a Danforth fund-raiser. After a few moments, she slipped out of the restroom and made for the gardens.

She had just taken a seat on a stone bench out of sight of the ballroom doors when a deep, masculine voice said, "You're not a ghost, are you?"

She turned with a startled laugh. "You sound disappointed."

A man materialized from the darkness. He was elegant in a dark tux with an equally dark collarless shirt, and the moonlight glanced off his dark hair. Her first thought was that he wore the clothing awfully well for an American. She immediately scoffed at herself. Just because she'd gotten used to Continental men, many of whom were pickier than women about their wardrobes and their facelifts, didn't mean she should be an equal snob. Still, this man had been born to wear a tux.

He said, "I am disappointed. I saw you flitting about the garden a few minutes ago in your white dress and I was sure you were the Twin Oaks ghost."

"Sorry." She shrugged, smiling. "I'm ordinary old flesh and blood."

"I wouldn't, by any stretch, call you ordinary," the man said.

His tone was warm and admiring and she was glad for the darkness because she felt herself blushing. She'd never been good at flirting, or the small talk men and women shared. Her deportment instructors had despaired of her socially. Her only saving grace was that she could dance like an angel.

She cleared her throat. "Were you making that up about the ghost?" She'd said it to divert him, but she really was interested.

"Absolutely not. May I join you?"

When she nodded, he straddled the bench on which she sat, facing her with an easy air. "Well over a hundred years ago, a young woman was kidnapped from her family's suite and ravished by a blackguard on the third floor of the hotel. She threw herself from the window and was killed. Legend has it that on a clear night, you can see her walking through the gardens, crying for her lost virtue."

Selene was fascinated. "And is there any truth to substantiate the legend?"

He nodded. "The hotel's records give her name and the date of her death, which has been confirmed with U.S. census records of the time. She's buried in a local cemetery."

"Do you know anyone who's ever seen her?" She cast a quick look around, not out of fear but curiosity.

"My paternal great-grandfather supposedly did. He was at a ball here in the nineteen-forties and he came out to the garden to wait for a girl who'd agreed to meet him there. He heard a woman's voice behind him but when he turned, he clearly saw what he described as "the shade of a young girl."

"'Shade' is a dated word for ghost," Selene mused.

"Exactly." Her storyteller nodded, his deep voice animated. *"He wrote down the whole account, with a great many more details and it's still in our family today. It's only one of about a dozen alleged sightings of the young lady."*

"No wonder you were disappointed," she said.

Perfect white teeth flashed as he smiled. *"Could I possibly retract those words? I'm not usually so gauche."*

She was charmed. *"Consider them erased."*

He pantomimed relief. Then he tipped his head to one side, studying her. *"You don't seem the least bit unnerved by that story."*

"You said she's sad, not dangerous," she pointed out. *"I'm sensible that way. Now if you were to take me to Bavaria, there's a certain castle you couldn't pay me to enter. The spirit who haunts the place was killed defending his family from a neighboring kingdom's warriors, and he's chased any number of visitors through the halls. One woman fell down the stairs and broke an ankle, and she swears she was pushed."*

He was nodding at her story. *"Vindictive ghosts are fairly common. Your accent isn't German,"* he said *thoughtfully, "but I'm willing to bet you've spent quite a bit of time in Europe?"*

She smiled. "You'd win the pot. I lived in Switzerland most of my youth before attending university in the U.K."

"So you're British."

"Oh, no, I'm American," she said. "Although I've only been home for five days."

His smile was wide and direct, his eyes too dark to name their color in the moonlight, but filled with an interest she couldn't miss. "And will you be staying for a while?"

"Yes." She returned the smile. If she'd ever met a man with such charisma before, she couldn't recall it.

There was a brief moment of silence while he held her gaze. She was aware of the singing insects around them, the sweet strains of orchestral music filtering from the ballroom.

"My flower garden ghost," he said in a husky tone. He rose and offered her a hand. "Would you like to dance?"

In response, Selene put her hand in his, feeling the strength in his fingers as he lifted her to her feet, the hard muscles of his arms as they went around her, the warm promise of his big body so close to hers. Clouds of butterflies rose in her stomach, making her hand tremble in his.

"Are you cold?" His voice was a rumble in his chest, his breath stirred the silky tendrils of hair near her temple. She realized that all she had to do was turn her head and lift her chin and his lips would be on hers.

It took all the willpower she had to prevent herself from doing exactly that.

* * *

"It was heavenly," she told Guillemette. "We danced for nearly an hour. We talked. He loves folklore, ghosts and local legends and such. He was just fascinating. And handsome, and so sweet…"

"So who is he? And what's happened since then?" Guillemette prodded her. "You said that was two months ago."

Suddenly, the pleasure drained from the day. "It was. And nothing's happened since."

"What? Why?" Her friend began to sputter in French, and if she hadn't been so upset, Selene would have laughed.

"Willi," she said, "don't you want to know what his name is?"

"Oui." Her friend's voice grew wary.

"Adam Danforth."

"Who's Adam Danforth?" Guillemette's response reflected her lack of comprehension.

"His father is running against mine for the senate," Selene told her. "My father would be furious if I got involved with his rival's son."

"Why?" Guillemette seemed to take it in stride.

"Because…" She floundered, unprepared for the question. "Because Father's very competitive. His political career means everything to him. He's constantly looking for scandal that he can leak about the Danforth family. He isn't—isn't always very nice." That was difficult for her to admit.

Guillemette's silence spoke volumes. Finally, she said, "Does this Adam know who you are?"

"Oh, yes. He sent me flowers the next day." The memory made her smile. "A beautiful arrangement with a note thanking me for the evening."

"And you…?"

"Sent him a thank-you note, of course," she said. "But you must see why I shouldn't see him again."

"I see nothing of the sort," her friend said, more than a little heat in her voice. "Selene, there is no rational reason why your father should mind you going out with this man. This is the twenty-first century, not the Middle Ages!"

"They don't exactly have a friendly rivalry," she said in a defensive voice as she recalled some of the more offensive tactics her father had resorted to recently. "It just wouldn't be that easy, Willi."

"Nothing good in life comes easy," Guillemette said firmly. "Look at me. I had to be vetted by the *queen*."

Selene laughed. "So tell me all about it. I'm dying for details. Did you curtsey correctly? What did her crown look like? Did you have to kiss the glove?"

Lea was going to kill him if he was late for lunch again. The thought of his petite half sister's eyes sparkling with ire made him grin as Adam Danforth breezed into D&D's with the weekly payroll envelopes. He handed them off to the manager of the coffeehouse, checked the mail and his messages, and rushed back out again.

He checked his watch. He might just make it. He'd made a habit of getting together with his newfound sibling once a week or so as she adjusted to being a part of the large and loud Danforth clan—

It was gone! He stopped inside the entryway, his cursory scan of the bulletin board halted. For weeks after he'd first posted the note, he'd checked that board several times a day. But as the days passed and he never heard another word from Selene Van Gelder, anticipation and hope had shriveled and died.

He'd given up on finding a woman who liked him for what he was—a dorky guy who liked to talk about history and ghost stories. He'd had women chasing him for years but none of them really wanted *him*. They wanted his family's prestige, they wanted his money, some of them even wanted his body, to which he honestly couldn't say he objected—but not one of them appealed to him on an intellectual level.

And then he'd found Selene.

He'd been amused by his mistake that night at the fund-raiser, and initially assumed she would find him quaint and rather boring just like every other woman. He'd launched into the ghost tale more to get rid of her than because he thought she would really be interested.

It was a technique he'd perfected over the years since he'd overheard Angela DuFrayne laughing at him. He'd actually dreamed of marrying Angela until he'd realized he was nothing more than a cash cow to her. And a boring one at that. He should probably thank her one day, he thought bitterly. She'd taught him what women really thought of him. These days, he got a perverse pleasure from seeing a woman's eyes glaze over after she thought she'd snagged herself a conquest. He supposed he had a really sick sense of humor.

But Selene had been different. He'd never seen her in the light so he wasn't sure, but he imagined her eyes were a deep, dark blue. She was pretty in an old-fashioned kind of way, with a demure presence and a surprising, delightful sense of humor. Her nose was small and straight, her lips full and bowed like a doll's and there was an irresistibly cute little cleft right in the center of her chin. Her heart-shaped face had been emphasized by her upswept hair, which left wisps of curl dancing along her cheeks and forehead. Those great big eyes had fastened on his face attentively, and within moments he'd forgotten he was boring old Adam, the dull Danforth brother.

They'd talked, and then he'd asked her to dance, feeling he had to get his arms around her or die trying. She'd fit into them as if she'd been made to rest there, with her head on his shoulder and her face turned into his neck, and he'd felt the small gusts of her breath warm on his throat. He'd wanted to kiss her, wanted it badly, but he'd sensed that she was as skittish as the high-strung mare he'd ridden while visiting his cousin Toby in Wyoming a year ago, so he'd restrained himself. The last thing he'd wanted to do was scare her away.

And then he'd asked her name.

"Van Gelder? Related to John?" He didn't have the acting ability to hide his shock. This beautiful young woman was related to that—that slimy piece of work?

Her little chin lifted defensively and the glittering earrings and necklace she wore sparkled in the moonlight. "His daughter."

He couldn't help it; he laughed. Of all the ridiculous coincidences…!

Her chin hitched even higher. "Care to share the joke?"

He stopped laughing. "I'm Adam Danforth."

She recoiled. There was no other word for it. "Danforth." It was so faint he barely heard her. "Oh, God."

She looked even more appalled than he'd felt a moment ago, and it irritated him. "Look," he said, "there's no reason our last names have to matter, right?"

She didn't answer.

"I want to see you again, Selene." He savored the unusual name. It suited her.

"No." Her voice trembled. "That wouldn't be wise."

"It can't be that big a deal," he said, feeling stupidly panicked. God, he'd just met the woman. "You're acting like we're the Hatfields and McCoys."

"More like the Montagues and the Capulets," she said, and he realized she wasn't kidding.

"Selene—"

"I have to go now." She took a step back, and her hand lifted. He felt small, cool fingers cup his jaw and rest along his cheek. "Thank you for a lovely evening, Adam. I'm sorry I can't see you again."

It wasn't until later that he'd wondered what she was doing at his father's fund-raiser, and then it was too late to ask.

Adam shook himself out of reminiscence, realizing he was still glued to the spot in front of the bulletin board. He'd tried to call her twice the day after the fund-raiser, but she hadn't been in either time, and he hadn't wanted to leave a message and get her in trouble with her father. He'd sent her flowers that same day, and then he'd left a note at the coffeehouse a few days after he'd received her very correct little thank-you note for the flowers. Her card had been so dry, so devoid of anything other than the barest social nicety, that he had finally realized that she truly didn't intend to contact him again.

He wasn't a stalker, and if she didn't want to see him, he had to respect that. But perhaps one day she'd read the message on the bulletin board and change her mind. Couldn't she see how perfect they were for each other?

Cautiously, he reached out and traced the writing on the small sheet of paper that had replaced his note. *The lovely flowers you sent have wilted, too. My thoughts of you haven't. Shall we meet?*

Shall we meet? Had he just died and gone to Heaven? It was signed "S." Could it really be her?

His heart was actually hammering with excitement. Slowly, he detached the little note, a million fragmented thoughts bombarding him. Should he call her? He whipped out his little cell phone, then realized he could hardly call her father's house and identify himself. Not after the way that jerk had treated his father, doing his damnedest to ruin Abe Danforth's good name. And that reminded him of how difficult her decision to leave the note for him must have been.

After a long moment, he decided not to rush her. It had taken her two months to make contact with him; the last thing he wanted to do was frighten her away again.

He took one of his business cards from his pocket and turned it to the blank side, reaching for the pen inside his suit coat.

So what if he was a few minutes late to lunch? The girl of his dreams had given him the high sign and his response had to be just right.

Two

Three days went by and every time her cell phone rang, she crossed her fingers, hoping she would hear Adam Danforth's deep tones through the connection. She didn't always keep her cell phone on since she got so few calls but since she'd pinned that message and her hopes up on that bulletin board, she'd been carefully charging it and keeping it with her.

But the call she was waiting for never came.

Maybe Adam hadn't gotten the new message, Selene thought. *Maybe it was a sign that this was a bad idea.*

And yet she couldn't convince herself to forget about him. Maybe it was simply that he didn't want to call her father's home. He had no way of knowing the number she'd left was for her personal cell phone.

She'd just take one little trip by the coffeehouse, she

decided, to make sure her note hadn't fallen off the bulletin board, or gotten hidden beneath others. And while she was there, she could add a line that the number she'd left was her cell phone number. That way, he would be able to reach her without concern.

But when she stopped in front of the bulletin board at D&D's, her note was gone. And in its place was a business-size card.

Her heart began to pound and her mouth went dry. Slowly, hardly daring to believe she might get to see him again, she reached up and plucked the little card from the bulletin board. Turning it over, she saw it was indeed Adam's business card, inscribed with the elegant D&D logo in gold.

Here was proof. It hadn't been just a dream, or a message meant for someone else that she had misunderstood. Adam wanted to see her again. Even after she'd dismissed him when he'd sent those lovely flowers, he still wanted to see her again. Her fingers shook, making the little card tremble as she read the note on the back.

To my flower garden ghost: Meet me in front of the statue in Oglethorpe Square on Monday at 3:00 p.m.

Monday? *Today* was Monday! And it was half-past one already. But…which Monday did he mean? Well, she supposed it didn't matter. Today or next Monday, she'd be there waiting both times. She was going to meet Adam.

She reread the message. Oglethorpe Square. Where in the world was Oglethorpe Square? She had to get a map of Savannah right away!

An hour later, she not only had discovered that Oglethorpe Square was only about five blocks from the Cotton Exchange, where the coffeehouse was located, but that Savannah's historic district was a fascinating place. The proximity of the square left her plenty of time to browse through some of the shops in the area.

Although it was September, Savannah was still hot during the day and everyone wore summer clothes. Thankfully, she'd worn a lightweight day dress of mossy-green today. It wrapped over her breasts and buttoned at the waist and she'd worn a chic pair of Italian sandals with a matching purse. Of course, she thought ruefully, very few tourists walked around dressed as she did. American style was so much more casual than she was used to! She imagined people passing her assumed she worked in one of the many businesses in the area.

She walked leisurely through the pretty old streets. Before reaching Oglethorpe Square, she came to another of the unique landmarks that dotted the historic district's grid of streets at regular intervals. This one was...Reynolds Square, she noted, consulting her map. It was extraordinarily lovely, with live oaks covered in moss shading the thick grass.

And surprise, there was yet another statue right in the center of the little square. Savannah could probably win a contest for the most historic statues in a given area. This statue depicted a man named John Wesley, and as she read the plaque, she saw that Mr. Wesley had been the founder of the Methodist Church. Goodness, she certainly had a lot to learn about Savannah's history. She felt guilty that her own mother's family had lived here for generations and yet she, Selene, knew virtually nothing about her native city.

As she continued through Reynolds Square, she saw a gorgeous theatre on her left. The Lucas Theater. Idly, she wondered if the building's inside was as stunning as its exterior. Walking on down Abercorn Street, she could see the next square two blocks away. And if her guide book was correct, that would be Oglethorpe Square.

The butterflies in her stomach intensified. She was afraid he wouldn't be there, afraid he *would*. She glanced at her watch as she approached. Only two-forty-five. Fifteen minutes to get her nerves under control.

As she approached the square, her gaze found the statue mentioned in Adam's note and she paused to read about it. Ah, James Oglethorpe landed along the river in 1733 and promptly proclaimed the area the thirteenth colony in the name of King George II. No wonder he got his own little park.

She looked around. Tourists strolled the pretty little green square and what traffic there was on the adjacent streets moved sedately. An old-fashioned carriage with large back wheels and a roof that folded down idled at the curb. A driver in period dress and a top hat controlled the two beautiful white horses that pulled the vehicle.

Then she saw a man climb down from the carriage. He spoke to the driver before he turned and began walking her way.

Her heart stopped. She couldn't breathe. *Adam.*

She didn't move, couldn't move as he approached, could only drink in the wonderful sight of his tall, broad-shouldered form in a dark Italian-cut suit and white cotton shirt open at the throat. He was smiling and the autumn sun turned his dark hair to gleaming ebony. Then he stopped in front of her.

"Selene." His voice was deep and warm, matching the expression on his face as he surveyed her. "I'm so glad you came."

"I—" She had to stop and clear her throat. "I just got your note today."

His dark eyebrows rose. "I was hoping you'd find it. I was prepared to come by here for several Mondays if I had to." His eyes had been leached of color in the moon-silvered garden. Now she saw they were an unusual hazel, shining almost amber in the sunlight. He offered her his arm. "Would you care for a carriage ride?"

She made a small sound of surprise. "That would be lovely." She took his arm and let him lead her to the carriage. Beneath the lightweight fabric of his suit jacket, his arm felt solid and muscular. When they reached the carriage, she turned to take his hand so she could step up on the box to get in, but instead Adam set his hands at her waist. Before she could more than suck in a startled breath, he had lifted her into the carriage.

Her hands grasped his biceps to steady herself. She looked at him from beneath her lashes, feeling ridiculously shy. "Thank you."

"It was my pleasure." His voice and accompanying smile told her he meant it. Then he swung himself up inside the little carriage.

With the roof up, the carriage was a small, intimate cave. Adam wasn't a huge man, probably no more than six feet, but since she was barely over five feet, he seemed enormous. "Would you like the roof down?" he asked her.

She hesitated. The sunshine might feel nice…but it was so hot it easily could be too warm. And then there was her deep-seated fear of being discovered… "No thank you. It's very pleasant this way."

He smiled and nodded and she realized he'd been hoping she wouldn't want him to fold back the top. He leaned forward. "Okay, driver."

"Would you like a tour as you ride, sir?"

Adam glanced at Selene questioningly.

She shook her head. "I think I'd rather just talk with you, if that's all right."

He smiled. "That's terrific." Turning to the driver, he called, "No tour, thanks. Just a leisurely drive." As the driver picked up the reins and clucked to the horses, the carriage lurched into a steady rhythm. Adam looked at her again. "Would you like a snack?" He lifted a small cooler he'd stashed beneath the seat. "Grapes, cheese and chilled shrimp with cocktail sauce. And sweet tea and fresh juices." He grinned. "I would have preferred wine, but I didn't think you'd appreciate it if we got arrested."

She nodded, making a rueful face. "Wouldn't that be awful?" First the carriage ride, then the snacks… "This is wonderful. You're so thoughtful."

He was smiling at her, but the smile faded as she spoke and he seemed to be searching her face. "All I've been able to think of is you," he said. "I was afraid you might never come to D&D's, and you'd never see my message."

"I was hoping that I might run into you if I went there," she confessed.

"I wanted to call but I know how you feel about…"

"I appreciate that," she said. "You can call and leave a message on that line from now on. It's my cell phone."

His eyes lit up. "All right."

He flipped up a special little tray table feature atop the cooler and spread out the food, and as they nibbled, they chatted. She learned that he had been privately educated and that he had a degree in marketing and management. She told him about studying the classics and Greek literature at Oxford. "I graduated last year and haven't decided what I want to do with my degree yet," she said.

"The night we met, you said you'd be staying in Savannah," he said.

"Yes, at least until Father's campaign is over."

There was a momentary lull in the conversation and they both concentrated on their food. There was bound to be some awkwardness, she reminded herself, given the topics that were certainly off-limits.

"Have you always lived in Savannah?" She made an effort to get past the moment.

"Yes. Our family home was built in the late-nineteenth century. It's east of the city, actually, not far from Tybee Island." He smiled wryly. "We have a few ties to the area."

"I do, too," she said, "although I know very little about it. My mother was from one of Savannah's oldest families."

"She's not living, is she?" he asked gently.

"No. I never knew her. She died when I was born. She was the last of her family." He probably already knew that, just as she knew he'd lost his mother in an automobile accident when he'd been a young child. The media gave political candidates very little privacy these days. She might have learned even more about him if she'd cared to, but she'd deliberately refrained from investigating Adam's life in more than a cursory manner. It felt too sneaky, somehow.

"My mother died when I was small, too," he said.

"I'm sorry." She was well acquainted with being motherless. Growing up with a father who had barely been able to stand the sight of her had made for a lonely childhood. "Do you remember her at all?"

"I have a few vague memories of her, but that's it. My oldest brother remembers her better than any of the rest of us."

"Goodness," she said. "Exactly how many of you are there?" She'd read a number of different Danforth names connected with the campaign over the past few months and had wondered how they were related to Adam. Adam, about whom she'd never stopped thinking.

"I've got three brothers and a sister. And a half sister, too. Although we just met last month. She didn't grow up with the rest of the tribe."

Her eyes widened. "I bet your household was lively."

A little of the warm light went out of his eyes. "Not really. We all were sent to boarding school at a young age."

"I attended boarding schools in Switzerland," she said. "Actually, school felt more like my home than this does."

"You didn't come home often?"

"No." She swallowed, remembering those years when she'd waited in vain for a holiday invitation from her father. "I was only in Savannah twice in twelve years."

"Our father never came to see us at school," Adam said, clearly assuming her parent had.

"Oh, mine didn't, either. He was so busy that he said it would be better if I just stayed in Europe. It would have been a long trip for very brief visits."

Adam looked sincerely shocked. "You saw your father twice in twelve years?"

She nodded, aware of how very odd that sounded. "But I loved school. I made some wonderful friends and I usually spent the holidays with one of them. I didn't miss home."

"I did." Adam's cheery manner sobered a bit more. "I hated being away from my family and being separated from my brothers. We also have three cousins we're very close to, and I missed them and my aunt and uncle like crazy. We always spent school holidays and vacations with them."

"What a big family!" She didn't like seeing him sad and she sought to distract him from the unpleasant turn the conversation had taken. "Where do you fit?"

He smiled again. "Smack-dab in the middle. I have two older brothers, Ian and Reid, one younger brother Marcus, my half sister Lea and my other sister Kimberly, who's the baby of the family. My cousin Jake is older, his brother Tobias is my age and Imogene is younger." A shadow crossed his face.

She was so tuned in to him that she sensed his mood

had suddenly changed. "What are you thinking? You look so sad."

"I am," he admitted. "I have another cousin, the youngest of all of us, who disappeared five years ago."

"Disappeared? Was she kidnapped?" It sounded like something off Court TV, something she'd discovered she loved watching since she'd come to the States.

"If she was, we've never been contacted with a ransom demand." Adam sighed. "She went to a rock concert with a friend. There was a miniriot and when everything was sorted out, her best friend was located in the hospital but Victoria, my cousin, was missing."

"What did the friend say? Surely she could tell you where your cousin went."

"She suffered some injuries." He shook his head. "Tanya never recovered any memory of what happened that night."

"Not ever? Sometimes things come back as people grow older."

He shrugged. "She's not still in the area, I don't believe. But if she'd remembered anything helpful, she would have contacted us. I hope. She wasn't exactly the most reliable person."

She was aghast. "But…people don't just *vanish*."

"That's what we thought, too." Adam seemed to shake himself. "Life goes on and we all want to believe there's still hope she'll turn up eventually, but some days it's harder than others to stay hopeful."

"I imagine it is," she said softly. Without thinking, she laid a comforting hand on Adam's arm. He immediately placed his free hand over hers and squeezed her fingers.

"I don't think about it every minute anymore," he said. "Sometimes I feel guilty for that, but another part of me realizes that the rest of us have to continue to live as normally as we can."

"Do you see your brothers and sisters and cousins often?"

He smiled again and she felt a sense of relief that her question had lightened his heart a little. "I see most of them at least once a week," he said. "And that's excluding all this campaigning that we're doing for Dad."

"I always thought it would be so much fun to have brothers and sisters," she said. "Do any of them live close?"

"They all do. And most of my cousins do, as well. I think I told you my cousin Jake and I co-own the D&D chain, so we work together every day. And then there's Jake's best bud Wes, who's sort of been unofficially adopted by the Danforth clan—"

"Gracious! How do you keep them all straight?"

He grinned. "When you grow up with it, I guess it's ingrained." Then he pointed to another of the lovely little squares they were passing. "See that big boulder? It marks the grave of a local Indian chief. This is Wright Square. It's named for James Wright, who was the last man to govern the colony of Georgia before the States became independent."

"I wish I knew a tenth of what you know about Savannah," she said.

"I could give you a moonlit walking tour of the haunted spots around the historic district some evening." He hesitated and she was surprised by the flash of vulnerability that she caught in his eyes. "If you think that would be interesting."

The conversation she'd overheard at the coffeehouse on her first visit rose to the surface of her memory, and she knew a surprising anger at the shallow women who had hurt this intelligent, interesting man. "It sounds fascinating," she assured him.

"How about tonight?"

Her face fell. "I can't. Daddy needs me to attend a fund-raiser at a place called the…the Crab Shack?" She smiled. "He told me to dress down. I have visions of a small one-room cabin with a latrine in the back."

Adam laughed. "The Crab Shack at Chimney Creek. It's informal but not *that* bad."

"You've dined there?"

"The food is excellent and it's very picturesque." He took her hand from where it still rested on his arm and linked her fingers with his. "How about tomorrow night, then?"

"Tomorrow evening would be fine," she said. "Where would you like me to meet you?"

"I could—" he began, but he stopped as she shook her head. "No," he said, "I guess picking you up is out of the question." He snapped the fingers of his free hand. "Could you meet me at about 6:45 at the ferry dock? There's a dinner cruise that begins at seven," he said. "It's two hours long and afterward we could walk for a while."

"That sounds lovely," she said. "Where is the ferry dock?"

He smiled. "I'm going to have to remember this city

is new to you." He squeezed her fingers. "That will give me an excuse to spend lots of time showing you around."

She was beautiful, Adam thought the following evening. He watched as she smiled and thanked the captain for the cruise. The man was at least two decades older than she was, but he sucked in his stomach and actually bowed over her hand with the silliest smile on his face that Adam had ever seen.

Adam figured he probably looked just as dazed when she smiled at him.

She'd been beautiful that evening in the garden, her white gown had seemed to glow in the moonlight, but it had been a dreamlike beauty, in gentle shades of shadow. At first he'd thought she was a ghost but in truth she'd looked more like an angel.

But yesterday, in vibrant Technicolor, she had come alive, her eyes not the blue he'd imagined but a deep, mossy, unforgettable green. Porcelain skin, roses blooming just beneath the velvety surface of her cheeks, her nose a pert little slope upon which he could barely resist dropping a kiss. Yesterday her hair had been down, floating around her shoulders, but tonight, like that first night, she'd worn her shining chestnut hair in a pretty twist in deference to the river breezes. She'd donned a nautical-themed skirt and top and she looked…perfect.

He gave up trying to find adequate words to describe her. As she turned and took his arm, she smiled at him and his heart gave a funny little leap. She seemed too good to be true. Beautiful, intelligent, great sense of humor, she even seemed to genuinely enjoy his penchant for spouting historical trivia and ghost stories. She was poised and confident enough to deal with the pressures of being a Danforth— *Whoa!* he cautioned himself. *Slow down. You haven't met a woman yet who likes the real you.* But in his heart, he didn't feel he was moving nearly fast enough.

"Thank you so much," she said. "No one should ever visit Savannah without taking a cruise on the river."

"And you didn't even get seasick," he said, smiling at her enthusiasm.

She smiled back, rather smugly. "I took motion sickness medication. Experience has taught me well."

"Aha," he said. "So you do have a flaw!"

Her eyebrows rose. "Plenty of them." She started to laugh, leaning her head against his arm, "But I don't plan to share them with you. Now where are we going on this walk?"

"We'll start with the pirate's house," he told her. "For years, rumor had it that a tunnel led from the rum cellar out to the river, and unsuspecting patrons of the tavern were sometimes drugged and carried aboard ships that needed a full complement of sailors. One Savannah policeman who stopped in for a drink woke up on a China-bound schooner. It supposedly took him two years to get home. Some people dismissed it until the tunnel was found during renovations."

"Can you imagine being one of those poor men conscripted in such a way?" she said. "And isn't this the building that Robert Louis Stevenson is said to have described in *Treasure Island*?"

"Yes!" He knew he sounded as astonished as he felt. And he felt the last of his doubts sliding away. "You're the first woman I've ever met who knew—or even cared about—a detail like that."

"Maybe you just haven't met the right women," she said, slanting him a shy smile.

"Until now." He gently removed her hand from his arm and then placed his arm around her, hugging her close to his side. "That's better."

"Yes," she said, letting her own arm slide around his waist. "It is, isn't it?"

They walked for nearly an hour as he regaled her with stories of Savannah's history and a few ghostly sightings as well. As they passed the birthplace of Juliette Gordon Low, the founder of the Girl Scouts and a building said to be haunted by the ghosts of two of Low's ancestors, she asked, "Have you ever seen one of these ghosts?"

"No," he said slowly. His family home immediately sprang to mind and he wondered if she'd think he was crazy if he told her. "I've never seen a ghost."

She hesitated and he realized she must be more tuned in to him than he expected when she said, "But you know someone who has?"

"My family's home is haunted," he said baldly. She might as well hear it all.

"By whom?" To his surprise, she didn't sound skeptical, but was very matter-of-fact.

"We don't know," he said. "Let me amend that. We

think it's the spirit of a governess named Miss Carlisle. She was hired by one of my ancestors in the early 1890s but on the night of her arrival, her carriage overturned on the road up to the house and she was killed. She was buried on the estate beneath a young oak tree."

"Poor girl." Selene sounded upset, as if they were speaking of someone they'd known. "Where was she from? Did her family ever learn her fate?"

"I don't know," he said. "I'm not sure anyone knew very much about her."

There was a short silence while they contemplated the fate of a young girl from an earlier age.

Finally, Selene said, "Who has seen her? And why do you believe it's her? This Miss Carlisle?"

"There were no sightings, no rumors of ghostly goings-on at Crofthaven until after her death. She was seen quite a few times during the twentieth century," he told her. "Every sighting was near the tree where she's buried. It's still there," he added belatedly. "One of my ancestor's guests described her dress in great detail and a historian confirmed that her apparel reflects turn-of-the-century clothing."

"How long has it been since anyone's seen her?" They had stopped walking altogether and she turned to face him, the smooth oval of her face tilted up attentively.

"That's the strange part," he said. "In the past nine months, she's been seen three times."

"Oh!" Selene rubbed her hands up and down her arms. "I've got goose bumps. Tell me all about them."

"Okay." He led her to a stone bench along the edge of a square they were passing and indicated that she should take a seat. As she did, he sank down beside her. "In February, Kimberly's fiancé saw her along the road. She tried to speak to him, but Zack couldn't figure out what she was saying. The way he tells it, she got ticked off just like any woman with a guy who doesn't get it, and left."

Selene smiled, and he could see the flash of her teeth in the dark that had fallen over the city. "I wonder what she was trying to tell him?"

"We don't know. She was seen again in May. This time, it was a houseguest—my sister-in-law's brother—and Dennis actually thought she was another guest who walked into the wrong bedroom. He didn't even realize who he'd seen until the next day."

"Goodness! Had she been seen in the house before?"

"No," he said. "That one was a shock to all of us. She came around again in July, and Lea's fiancé saw her this time. He swears she kept saying something that sounded like 'farther' or 'father.'"

Selene was shaking her head. "Poor thing. I hope someone can help her find whatever it is she's looking for one of these days."

"So do I," he said. "She does no harm wandering around, except for startling a few people. But I think there must be something specific she wants, or wants to communicate or find."

"I wonder if there's any significance to the fact that recently she's been seen only by houseguests or people who aren't related by blood to the Danforths," she said.

Adam stared at her. "I missed that completely," he said slowly. "You're right. I may have to go back through some of the older accounts to see if the folks who had a sighting were family."

"Blood relatives," she clarified. "Not people who married into the family."

"Blood relatives," he echoed. He took her hand. "Thank you. I guess it seems silly but it's been bugging me, the thought that she's so unhappy."

"It doesn't seem silly at all," Selene said gently. "It seems thoughtful. And caring."

Was that what she really thought? Warmth spread through his chest and he leaned forward, taking both her hands in his. "I'm so glad you agreed to see me again."

Her eyelids lowered. "I shouldn't have, I know. If my father finds out…"

"Why don't you take me to meet him?" Adam said. "Then we won't have to sneak around and you won't have to worry. The election is only two months away. As long as we keep it low-key until then, surely he won't mind."

"Adam, you don't understand." Her fingers had tensed in his. "My father doesn't—he wouldn't understand. If he finds out I'm seeing you, he'll forbid it."

He tried to smile, although the certainty in her tone had his stomach curling into a knot. "Surely it isn't that bad. I could—"

"No!" she said. "You can't do anything. Or I won't see you again." She tugged her hands from his and rose, clearly agitated.

Adam sat very still, looking at her rigid spine. He didn't know what to say. He hated feeling as if they had to watch over their shoulders every moment.

Then she turned, and he could see the track of a single tear shining in the moonlight as it streaked down her cheek. "I don't want you to be unhappy with me," she whispered. "I just know that until this election ends and Daddy settles down, he's not going to be able to deal with me dating a Danforth."

"All right." He rose and went to her, taking her into his arms. She felt small and soft against him, and when she wrapped her arms around his neck and let her body rest trustingly along his, he thought his heart might just burst right out of his chest. "We'll do it your way. Just promise me you won't let your father stop you from seeing me."

"Of course not." She drew back and looked up at him. "You're the best thing that's ever happened in my life, Adam."

He drank in her stunning features, the appeal in her wide eyes, and he was lost. "As you are in mine." And then he bent his head and found her mouth with his.

Three

She was lost the moment his lips touched hers. Adam's mouth was warm and gentle as he kissed her, cajoling her to return the kiss. His arms were hard and muscular and yet he held her as though she were made of crystal.

With a murmured sound of pleasure, she ran her palms up his arms to his shoulders and gave herself to the sweetness of the moment.

After a moment, he drew away. "When can I see you again?"

"Soon," she said dreamily, feathering her fingers through the soft hair at the back of his head.

He kissed her again. "Tomorrow."

Immediately, she felt a return of the dread that hovered in the back of her mind, the fear that her father might find out. She was usually home much of the time. He might get suspicious if she suddenly was busy every moment.

"The day after tomorrow," she said. "Tomorrow's a little crowded." It was a lie, but she wasn't going to take any chances.

"All right," he agreed. "Lunch? Meet me in Oglethorpe Square where we met the other day."

She smiled, relieved at his easy acceptance. "All right. Could we go somewhere outside the city to eat, though? I'd like a change of scenery." And then there would be no chance of running into anyone either of them knew.

She didn't get home until nearly eleven, and she let herself in quietly, hoping her father was asleep already. But as she tiptoed toward the grand staircase that led to her suite of rooms on the second floor, he appeared in the doorway of his study.

"Selene! I was beginning to wonder where you'd gotten to." He switched on the large chandelier that hung in the entrance and she blinked in the sudden bright light.

John Van Gelder looked tired. And…old, she thought. Older than a man of sixty-three should look. Even the silver that had replaced his blond hair in places seemed tarnished and dull. His dress shirt ballooned over the waistband of his creased linen slacks, poorly concealing his girth. She'd been a little shocked to see how much weight her father had put on compared to her memory of him.

"Hello, Father."

"Out on the town, I suppose? You do realize that your actions will attract the attention of every reporter, don't you?" His pale gray eyes were as sharp as his tone.

"Yes, Father. I took a tour of the historical district." That wasn't a lie. Exactly. Not like what she'd said to Adam about being busy tomorrow.

"At night?"

"It focused on ghosts and legends. Did you know that there really was a girl who stood where the statue of the Waving Girl is? She waved a cloth over her head just like the statue is depicted to signal boats on the river, and some people swear they've seen the stone cloth of that statue ripple as well."

John snorted. "There's a ghost associated with practically every old building in Savannah. You're nobody if your home isn't haunted in this city." He chuckled at his own wit. Then he sobered abruptly. "Did you catch the interview with Abe Danforth tonight?"

Silently, she shook her head. *Danforth.* She felt as if the name were written in black marker on her forehead.

He smiled grimly. "Cable news. They had him scrambling to explain why his kids spend more time with their aunt and uncle than they do with him. Rumor has it his own kids can't even stand him. And I wonder how they feel about a bastard half sister?"

Appalled at her father's coarseness and lack of empathy, Selene shook her head. "I imagine it's a difficult time for them."

"I hope so," her father said with relish.

Not for the first time, she wondered what her mother had been like. Why she had married John Van Gelder.

Had he been kinder, gentler, more *human* once? He'd been handsome as a younger man, though time and temperament had taken away most of his good looks and left him looking calculating and less than pleasant. "Father," she said suddenly, "how did you and my mother meet? What was it about her that you fell in love with first?"

Her father went still. Every muscle in his body froze. "Why would you bring that up?" he asked, a fleeting expression of anguish twisting his features before he wiped it away.

"I know nothing about her, nothing about her family," she said. "I just wondered…"

"Well, don't wonder," he said abruptly. "There's no sense in talking about the past." He swallowed, then, almost reluctantly, he added, "You look like her, you know. Damn near a dead ringer."

"I do?" She was thrilled. "Do you have any pictures of her?"

To her surprise, her father didn't answer. In fact, he didn't even appear to hear her. As she'd been speaking, he had turned and disappeared into his study again, his shoulders slumped, his eyes unfocused.

Slowly, she turned and made her way up the stairs, treading lightly on the lovely runner that echoed the soft colors in the upstairs hall. Unless she was very much mistaken, her father was still grieving for her mother. Still! After twenty-three years, he could hardly bear to speak of her.

And another realization swept over her as his words echoed in her ears. *You look like her, you know. Damn near a dead ringer.* She, Selene, reminded him of what he'd lost.

As she entered her suite, decorated in subtle shades of lavender and spring-green with dainty, feminine touches provided by an interior designer, her eyes began to sting and a true feeling of hopelessness crept into her soul.

All these years she'd told herself her father was merely busy, a single man with a political career who probably thought boarding school was the best option for his only child. But now she had to face the truth. Her father had sent her away deliberately. Because he couldn't stand to have her around, reminding him of what he'd lost.

A sob hitched her breathing and she bit down hard on her lower lip to contain others. Her father didn't love her. Didn't want her. The only reason he'd brought her home, she saw, was because her presence was good for his image in this campaign.

Another sob threatened and she swallowed it, nearly choking on the lump in her throat. She would *not* cry, she told herself fiercely. She didn't need her father. He'd never allowed that.

But now…now she had Adam. The ache in her chest lessened a little and she focused on thoughts of him, of the warmth in his striking amber eyes when he smiled at her. Unless she was completely reading him wrong, he was feeling the same things she was. Attraction, both physical and intellectual. He made her laugh. Made her think. Made her wonder at the strength of the desire that had swamped her when he'd kissed her tonight.

She wanted him to kiss her again. Soon. Wanted more

of the magical sensations he sent racing through her system. She hugged thoughts of him to her and carefully avoided thinking of her father, of the hurt he'd inflicted on her over the years. In two days, she would see Adam again.

The two days took forever to pass. Every minute seemed to have hours built into it.

But finally, *finally,* she stepped out of the taxi and walked into Oglethorpe Square, and there he was.

He was dressed in a finely woven patterned sport shirt and khaki pants and his eyes lit up when he saw her walking toward him. No, they didn't light up so much as they caught fire, she amended, her heart skipping madly at the heat that blazed a trail over her short, flirty sundress and finally landed on her mouth.

He opened his arms as she reached him, and when he drew her to him for a kiss, she couldn't have objected if she'd tried. All she could do was wrap her arms around his wide shoulders and kiss him back, delighting in his obvious pleasure.

When a passing tourist whistled at them, Adam chuckled and loosened his arms. "I can think of better places to be doing this," he said, smiling. "Good afternoon."

"Good afternoon," she repeated, unable to prevent a silly smile from curving up her own lips. How could he make her so happy with one little kiss?

He took her hand and led her to a sporty little American car. "I thought we could drive over to Hilton Head for lunch," he said. "It's less than an hour away, and it's a pretty drive."

He could have taken her to the moon for all she cared,

as long as she could be with him. On the drive out, he regaled her with stories of the area through which they were passing. They lunched at a charming little restaurant by one of the Savannah River's last fingers before it reached the sea. Their waiter showed them to a table on a shaded deck and brought them steaming plates of lobster with dishes of butter. There were white aprons to protect their clothes and Adam teased her about setting a new fashion when the apron extended below the hem of her dress, making it look as if she wore nothing beneath the apron. They cracked lobster claws, drank a bottle of white wine, and once again she realized how comfortable she was with him.

"Tell me about growing up in Europe," he said after he'd finished telling her about Hilton Head Island's evolution into a golf mecca. "You must be getting tired of hearing me talk."

"Not at all," she assured him.

"Well, *I'm* getting tired of hearing myself," he said, grinning. "Your turn. Where was your school?"

"There were two, actually," she said. "I began in Zurich and was there for seven years. My best friend was French, and when her family decided to transfer her to a school in Geneva for secondary school, I begged Daddy to do the same. After I finished, I attended Oxford. What else do you want to know?"

"Which country did you like better?"

"Switzerland," she said promptly. "It's far too dreary in England to suit me."

"What did you study at Oxford?"

"Classical languages and Greek literature."

"So you speak other languages?"

Her eyebrows rose. "Well, I spent a lot of time with my friend Willi's family on holiday, so I learned French quite young. I'm also fluent in German—it's hard not to be when it's one of the national languages the Swiss speak. Other than that, I've studied Latin. But that's a dead language, of course."

Adam laughed. "I've always thought that sounded so morbid. Wouldn't it be better to say, 'languages that have passed away,' or, 'deceased languages'?"

Now it was her turn to laugh.

While she was still chuckling, he said, "When I met you I thought you had an interesting accent. Now I know why."

"I don't have an accent," she said indignantly. "Not like y'all do." The sentence was a perfect imitation of a slow Savannah drawl.

"There you go," said Adam. "Now you sound normal."

She was about to answer him when she caught sight of a familiar face. She froze.

Two tables away, one of her father's chief campaign workers was being seated at a table with three other men. She couldn't see the faces of the others, so she had no way of knowing whether or not she might recognize them also.

Immediately, she shifted sideways so that Adam's body was blocking her from view. "Adam," she said in a low voice. "Don't turn around, but there's a man behind you who knows me. He's working on my father's re-election and I've spoken to him several times at events."

Adam's eyebrows rose. He had rinsed his fingers

with lemon and he laid aside the napkin with which he was drying them. "And you're sure that telling your father about us is such a terrible thing?" His voice was very neutral, very careful and she realized she had hurt him with her insistence on hiding their meetings.

She leaned across the table, searching for words to explain. "My father has spent his whole life in politics. This race is terribly important to him…. If he—I don't know what will happen if he doesn't win. I don't think he's ever even imagined what life without politics would be like."

"There are a lot of other ways to contribute to the democratic process than by being an elected official." For the first time since they'd met, his eyes were cool and distant, and she couldn't tell what he was thinking.

"You don't know my father," she said in a small voice.

There was a brief, tense silence at the table.

"Well," he said at last. "If you're so eager to get out of here, we may as well go."

He rose and came around the table to pull out her chair. She noticed that he stayed between her and the man she had recognized as much as he could, and she used the opportunity to duck her head and put on the huge dark sunglasses she had with her.

Shortly afterward, he handed her back into the car and they set off for Savannah again. She'd expected it to be a long and painfully quiet drive, but Adam began to tell her stories of some of the scrapes he, his siblings and his cousins had gotten into when they were all younger. She was fascinated and her imagination ran wild trying to picture being part of such a tribe of children. She told him of school escapades, though they generally were much milder than some of the tales Adam had to tell. She enjoyed it so much that she forgot the change in his behavior over lunch, forgot the disagreement, if that's what it even had been, that they'd had.

But when they'd parked, Adam turned to her and said, "Are you going to see me again?" and his face was so sober that the constraint between them earlier immediately returned in a rush.

"I—I'd like to," she said. "I'd really like to. If you want."

"Of course I want to see you," he said. He picked up her hand and lightly rubbed his thumb over the knuckles, then raised it to his mouth and pressed a kiss to the back of her hand. "I wish we didn't have to sneak around behind your father's back, but I respect your concerns. But after the election, no more stalling. No matter what the outcome of the election, we tell him. Agreed?"

She nodded, huge butterflies taking wing in her stomach and making her feel oddly breathless. "Agreed." Happiness rose in a steep, giddy rush. The election was still weeks and weeks away.

Weeks and weeks in which Adam clearly assumed they would still want to be together. She couldn't think of anything that would make her happier.

He drove out to Crofthaven after dropping Selene off at the edge of the historic district where she said she intended to take a cab. Ian had called earlier in the morning and asked him to meet him at the Danforth family mansion at four.

He parked in front of the palatial estate a short time later, barely noticing the grandeur of his family home. He thought about the ghost sightings every time he drove onto the property lately. And since his father's campaign had begun, he'd driven out here a whole lot more than he normally did.

"What do you want?" he murmured. "Can I do anything to help you?" Was it significant that she'd been seen inside the house, as Selene had wondered? Even when he was a child, he'd been enthralled by the stories of ghostly visitations in his home. Oddly enough, he'd never been afraid. He could remember waiting at windows, sneaking out after dark on the rare occasions he'd spent time at home, hoping for a glimpse of the ghost. But he'd never caught so much as a flicker of another presence.

"Hey, my partner!" His cousin Jake stood on the front steps waving at him, suitcoat slung carelessly over one shoulder.

Adam felt a rush of affection. Jake. Slightly taller, seriously broader through the shoulders, the two men still resembled each other enough that people often assumed they were brothers rather than cousins. Only a year apart, they had been buddies since childhood, often uniting against the older or the younger kids when squabbles arose. It had seemed natural for them to go into business together. Jake had approached him about it even before he'd graduated from college, and they'd begun planning immediately. Then Adam's older brother Ian wanted a piece of the action, although he hadn't wanted in on the operation. He'd offered to go in as a silent partner, and the combined investment of the three of them had paid off handsomely, thanks to Jake's and Adam's hard work. He was proud of D&D's, proud of what they'd accomplished.

"What's up?" he responded rhetorically to the greeting. He'd just seen Jake in a meeting yesterday before they'd gone their separate ways to check on various arms of their corporation.

"Don't know," Jake said as Adam reached him and they climbed the steps together. "Ian called and asked me to come out."

"Me, too." Adam puzzled over it for a moment. "Guess we'll find out in a minute. How's my man Peter doing?" he asked. Peter was Jake's four-year-old son, a son of whom he'd just become aware earlier in the year when Jake's old college friend Larissa had been forced to reveal their son's existence to Jake before a reporter did. A reporter who'd gone on the trail of Danforth dirt the moment the campaign was announced.

"He's good," Jake said and the warmth and pride in his tone dissolved Adam's moment of annoyance. "The asthma seems to be under control for the moment, and he's been bugging me to take him fishing again."

Adam chuckled. "So you're adapting well to fatherhood."

Jake grinned in response as he pushed open one of the massive doors. "Well enough that we're considering giving Peter a sibling one of these days."

They stopped inside the massive foyer, letting their eyes become accustomed to the lower light. It was cool and comfortable, but as always, Adam felt like a stranger there.

Not unwelcome, exactly. More…unnoticed. Just as he had when he was a child and his father had been too busy for any of his offspring.

Then a head peered out from around the door of the library, several yards down the main corridor. "You coming in here anytime soon?"

"Hello to you, too, Ian," said Adam with mock sarcasm. "Awfully good to see you."

His oldest brother grinned and Adam and Jake approached. "And even better to see the two of you, you money-making machines."

Jake made a rude noise. "Takes one to know one."

"You got that right." Ian held the door wide and beckoned them in. "Anybody want a drink?"

Adam shook his head. "No, thanks."

Jake eyed Ian speculatively. "Am I going to need one?"

Ian shrugged as the three men took seats in the club chairs in one corner. "Maybe."

"Why are we meeting *here?*" Adam said, making a gesture that encompassed their surroundings.

"Because this is one of the few places I'm certain is private and hasn't been bugged." Ian took a deep breath. "I've got a bad feeling about this Colombian corporation."

Adam sat forward. "The same one that tried to intimidate you into buying our coffee beans from their recommended sources by blowing up your offices?"

"And the same one we think was behind Marcus getting questioned by the police in June," added Jake. Marcus was Ian and Adam's younger brother, a lawyer for the family firm run by Ian.

"The same," Ian confirmed. "They're still trying to dictate to me. They've hinted that there will be more trouble for Marc if I don't cooperate."

"Hell." Jake stood and stalked to the window. "What are you going to do?"

Ian shrugged. "I don't think there's a lot I *can* do. But I can't give in. I'm positive the legal side of that business—the coffee bean business—is just a front for drug and money-laundering activities."

"So what do you want us to do?" If there was anything Adam could do to protect his younger brother, he'd do it.

"I don't know." Ian sighed. "I just want you to be aware that something could happen. Be on the lookout for anything weird or unusual."

Jake turned from the window and rolled his broad shoulders beneath the white dress shirt he wore. "Have you told Marc?"

Ian nodded. "We talked this morning. He's still pretty shaken by those questions about racketeering that got thrown at him in June."

"I bet." Adam stood, too. "I don't know about you, Jake, but I've changed my mind about the drink."

The men talked for another quarter hour, tossing around information and ideas, but no great strategies came to mind.

"We have to handle this carefully," Adam reminded

them. "Ian can't be implicated in anything illegal. It would blow Dad's campaign right out of the water."

"Yeah, but if Marcus gets in trouble, the end result is the same," Jake reminded them.

"God, I wish I knew how to resolve this," Ian said. "I can't go to the authorities. It would leak, and can't you just see the headlines?"

"Yeah," Adam said, bitterness rising as he thought of his own experience being the target of a media manhunt a decade earlier. "You're guilty until you're proven innocent."

"Danforth Son Allegedly Involved In Drug Deal," said Jake. "Drug Cartel Controlling Danforth Family? They skate right on the edge of libelous language without going far enough to get nailed."

"Exactly," said Ian.

The brothers and their cousin talked for a few minutes longer, then Ian said, "I wish I had something more specific to go on, but there's nothing I can pin down." He rose and Adam rose as well.

"We'll keep our eyes open," Jake promised, moving away from the window.

As they walked into the foyer, the front door opened and a shaft of sunlight fell across the marble floor. Abraham Danforth stepped into the room and stopped short when he saw the three younger men.

"Well," he said, "this is a surprise. Ah, welcome."

"Hello, Dad." Ian's voice was cool. "We borrowed your library for a meeting. We're just leaving."

"It's your home, Ian," Abe said. "You can use the library any time you like."

"Thank you."

There was an awkward silence. Abe said, "Hello, Adam."

"Hello, Dad." It was an echo of Ian's greeting.

"Hi, Uncle Abe." Jake cleared his throat. "I've got to get going. I promised Larissa I'd cook tonight."

"We've all got to go," said Adam. "Tell Nicola to call if you need us at any campaign functions in the next few weeks."

"All right. Thanks."

Adam thought his father's voice sounded wistful but he wasn't about to stick around and find out. He and his old man had never had a single conversation of any consequence that Adam could recall. It was hard to have *any* conversation with a father who was either traveling all the time or too busy for his kids. Why start now?

As the front door closed with a heavy thud behind them and they started down the steps, Ian shot a look at Jake. "You're *cooking?*"

"I'm a good cook," Jake said defensively. "Besides, if I want to get out of the house to play soccer on Saturday, I have to help out during the week."

Adam chuckled. "Aha. The truth comes out."

Ian was grinning, too. "Sounds like Katie's been giving Larissa pointers on how to manage a husband." Both Ian and Jake had only been married a few months.

"Give Katie a kiss for me and tell her hello," Adam said to Ian.

"With pleasure." Ian's eyes lit up with warmth at the mention of his wife and Adam stared at his older brother for a moment. Would he ever be that transparently in love with anyone?

Selene. Her face was in his head even before the thought had passed. *Whoa,* he thought. *There's no point in even thinking long-term until this stupid election is over.* He thought of her expression when she mentioned her father. He might not particularly enjoy his, but he certainly didn't have those conflicted emotions that she so clearly did. What had the man done to her to make her resent him and yet feel compelled to obey him?

"…and give this to Peter," Ian was saying to Jake as Adam tuned back in to the conversation. His older brother withdrew a small package of candy from his pocket and handed it to their cousin.

Jake laughed. "Larissa will kill me—and you."

"Then you'd better not let her catch you," Adam said.

Four

The tennis match was vicious. Adam was dripping with sweat as he walked to the net and shook hands with his opponent, a player from the country club with whom he had a match every other week from April through October. Then he turned and walked to the door leading off the tennis courts, a warm feeling of anticipation burgeoning within him.

Selene stood just outside the fence. She had arrived in time to watch the final set of the match and Adam knew a sense of satisfaction that he had beaten his buddy six-love that time.

"Hi," he said, taking her hand. He wanted to kiss her, wanted it badly, but he was conscious of his less-than-enticing appearance. "I'm glad you could make it. Do you mind waiting while I grab a quick shower? I stink."

She smiled. "I don't mind at all."

"I'll hurry." He squeezed her hand, wishing he didn't have to let go. "Did you have any place special in mind for lunch?"

She shook her head. "Wherever you like."

"Okay. You can sit on that bench while you wait. I'll be right back." He'd called her yesterday on her cell phone and invited her to have a picnic lunch with him after his match. It pleased him that she'd come a little early and watched him play.

With a final wave, he entered the building where the locker rooms were located. Stowing his equipment, he rushed through a shower and dressed, then headed back outside.

He smiled as he saw her still seated on the bench where he'd left her. She was so lovely—

"Adam! Hey, what's happening?"

He turned automatically as he recognized Jake's voice. From the corner of his eye, he saw Selene get to her feet.

"Hey, Jake." His expression warmed as he saw his cousin's best friend, Wes Brooks, as well. Wes had lived with Uncle Harold's family when they were teens and was practically another cousin. "Wes. How's married life treating you?"

"Excellent," Wes answered, gripping the hand Adam extended. His dark skin gleamed with chestnut highlights and his teeth were a white slash in his dark face. "You're soon going to be outnumbered by us happily married folks."

Selene's face flashed through Adam's mind. "You never know," he said. He wanted to turn and beckon to her to join them, wanted to introduce her to his family so badly he could almost taste it. But he knew how upset she would be, so he forced himself not to even glance her way.

"What's that supposed to mean?" Jake demanded, alert to Adam's cryptic comment.

"He's got a lady," Wes proclaimed. "Adam has found himself a woman, my friend."

"Okay, spill." Jake punched him lightly in the shoulder. "You can't keep a secret like that from us."

"Wanna bet?" Adam grinned. Then a couple walking toward the clubhouse caught his attention and the smile faded. "Oh, hell, there's Dad."

Jake and Wes both turned.

"He's got Nicola with him," Jake observed. "Maybe you can sneak away—"

"Adam!" For the second time in a few minutes, his name was called.

Slowly, he turned fully to face his father, wishing he had, indeed, been able to sneak away. "Hi, Dad. Hello, Nicola."

"Hey, Uncle Abe, Ms. Granville. You remember Wesley Brooks?"

"Of course." Nicola smiled as she shook Wes's hand, although Adam thought she looked distracted. "Good to see you."

"Are you two having lunch?" Jake asked and Adam silently blessed his cousin for initiating the small talk. He never knew what to say to his father. Consequently, there were a lot of awkward silences when they met.

"Yes," said Abe.

"No," said Nicola at the same instant.

The couple looked at each other and immediately looked away again. Adam was astonished to see a faint rise of red color climbing his father's neck, while Abe's normally unflappable campaign manager was looking everywhere but at her candidate.

"Ooo-kay." Adam gestured toward the court, simply for the sake of having something to say. "I just finished a match."

"And we just arrived to begin one." Jake made a show of checking his watch. "Wes, we're going to miss our time if we don't hurry."

Wes nodded. "We'd better go." He extended a hand first to Abe, then to Nicola. "Good luck with the campaign."

Jake followed his lead, giving his uncle and Nicola a hasty handshake. It was clear to Adam that the two men had picked up on the odd tension between the pair and didn't want anything to do with it. He couldn't blame them.

There was a brief, uneasy silence in the wake of their departure. Adam searched for something to say. But what was there to say to a man who'd been around so rarely during your childhood that you barely knew him?

"Adam," said Nicola, "I have a list here of some upcoming events we'd like you to attend." She balanced her briefcase in one arm and set her hand on the latches, but when Abe's hand came down over hers, she froze, still looking down at the satchel.

"We can get those to you later," said his father.

"That's fine." He tried to ignore the way Nicola stepped a pace away from Abe, but he wondered just what in hell was going on. "Just stick 'em in the mail or fax them to my office. I'll show up at whatever you want."

"I really appreciate your help," his father said. "Would you like to join us for lunch?"

"We're *not* having lunch," Nicola said, her face darkening as she looked up at Abe. "I told you I won't be staying."

"Ah, thanks, but I already have plans," Adam demurred. Jeez, *what* was going on with these two? "In fact, I'm running a little late myself."

"We won't keep you then," his father said. He opened his mouth as if to say something else, but then closed it again without speaking. "It was good seeing you, son."

A similar response was in order. But as his father hesitated and the silence grew again, he couldn't bring himself to echo the words. "I, ah, I'll be at those events you mentioned." He directed the words to Nicola.

"Thank you." She nodded once at him and moved on.

Abe looked after her, then back at Adam. "I'd better go." And he strode off after her.

Adam stood where he was. Okay, that had been weird. Really, really weird. Was he imagining it, or was his father personally involved with his campaign manager? Or maybe he wanted to be?

He shook his head as the two disappeared inside the clubhouse, then turned toward Selene. He was more than ready to get out of here and find a quiet spot to picnic with her.

The bench where she'd been sitting was empty.

His heart sank. Glancing around, he realized that she

hadn't simply moved farther away. She was nowhere to be seen. Frustration rose. Was she going to cancel on him?

He wanted to see her, dammit!

Whipping out his cell phone, he punched the button that would automatically dial her cell number. He'd programmed it in the very day she'd told him it was her personal number. The line rang once, then twice. And then someone answered.

"Hello?" Selene's voice sounded slightly breathless.

"Why did you run off?"

"I saw your father. And Nicola Granville. I was afraid one of them might recognize me."

"And that would have been the end of the world?" he demanded. The moment he said it, he was sorry. The last thing he wanted to do was upset her.

She didn't say anything.

He sighed, not caring if she could hear him. "My family isn't full of ogres. Okay, my father's a little clueless when it comes to how to be a father, but he's not—"

"It's not *your* family, Adam." Her voice sounded thick, as though she was on the verge of tears.

"If you won't even let your father meet me, how can you predict what he's going to do?" he demanded. "Selene, I—"

Love you. He caught the words just in time, as shocked as she undoubtedly would be if he'd said them aloud.

Holy hell. He was falling in love with her. Despite the awkwardness of their family situations, she was the woman whose face sprang to mind when someone talked about marriage. Marriage! Good God, he barely knew her.

But as he thought of the discussions they'd had, the interest she'd shown in the things that he enjoyed sharing with her, the gentle smile that lit her face when she first caught sight of him, he realized that deep inside, where it counted, his heart recognized its other half.

Years ago, he'd thought he was in love with Angela. But he'd created an ideal image in his mind that had been nothing like the self-centered, shallow reality. Selene, he knew, was the real thing.

"Adam?" Her voice was tentative. "I'm sorry. I didn't mean to hurt you. It's just that…we have to wait until the election is over. I don't want to do anything that might affect my father's campaign."

He couldn't see how the two of them being together would have any impact one way or the other on either of the candidates, but she sounded so desperate that he couldn't disagree. "All right," he said soothingly. "I promised you we'd wait, so we'll wait. But the day after this damned election is over, we're visiting both your father and mine and announcing our— our relationship."

"Okay. Thank you." Again, she sounded as if she might be crying.

"Where are you?" he asked. "I promised you a picnic and I never break my promises."

She laughed, a small, precious sound that lodged squarely in his heart. "I'm waiting in the little garden near the parking lot.

He couldn't see the parking lot from where he was standing. "Don't move. I'm on my way."

* * *

The next day was Sunday. When they'd finally had their picnic yesterday in one of the city's pretty squares, Adam had asked her to go out to Tybee Island with him.

She went to church with her father, then headed straight for her room to pack a bag. Her bathing suit went underneath her clothing. She grabbed a beach towel, sunscreen, her small bag of toiletries so she could shower off if she needed to afterward and went down to see if the cab she'd called had arrived.

"Where are you going?" Her father came down the hallway from the kitchen. "Lunch will be served soon."

"I told them not to set a place for me," she answered, turning to look at herself in the large gilded mirror over the marble-topped table in the foyer. "I'm going to the beach."

"You were gone all afternoon yesterday."

She turned, exasperation rising. She'd come home to help with his campaign. He'd never cared before where she was unless he needed her; in fact, he'd made it plain he didn't want her underfoot constantly. Maybe that was it. "What did you need me for?" she asked politely. "You could have called and left a message on my phone."

"I just wondered where you were," he said in a quarrelsome tone.

"I had lunch downtown and then I went shopping," she said, summoning her most reasonable tone. That was true enough. She *had* gone shopping after the luncheon picnic. "Do you need me for something today?"

Her father eyed her from beneath brows drawn together in a fierce line. "No," he said shortly. "Not today."

A horn beeping out front saved her from further interrogation.

"All right," she said. "Then I'm off to the ocean for the day. I don't know when I'll be back."

As the cab carried her to the little restaurant where she'd arranged to meet Adam, she wondered what her father would do if he found out who she was involved with. It almost seemed sometimes as if he hated Abe Danforth, but she couldn't imagine why. Adam's father seemed to be a middle-of-the-road candidate whose military service would make him look attractive to the voters. He'd never done anything heinous or illegal, and although there was one irrefutable instance of an extramarital affair, it was hardly shocking enough to ruin him. According to recent media reports, Abe had been surprised to learn that he'd left a daughter behind after his service in Vietnam and was intent on helping her fit into his family here. What would it be like to find out you had a sister you'd never known existed?

Adam was waiting by his parked car when she stepped out of the cab. She wanted to run to him and throw herself into his arms, but she contented herself with a warm smile as he touched her elbow. "Hello."

"Hi." He saw her into the car, then came around to his side. "Are you ready to head for Tybee Island?"

"More than ready. I adore the beach."

He shot her a surprised look. "Have you vacationed at the ocean regularly?"

"Not with my father," she said, understanding his confusion. "My best friend from school is French. Her family frequented the Riviera and since she was always dragging me home on holiday with her, I went along."

"The Riviera." Adam's eyebrows rose. "The Atlantic coast is beautiful but I'm not sure it can compete with that."

"Is there sand? Surf? Sun?" She grinned at him, her spirits soaring. "It will do just fine if it has those things."

"This is a good time of year to visit," he told her. "The summer is over and most kids are back in school so there are a lot fewer tourists around."

He was right, she saw when they arrived.

The beach was wide and white, and medium-sized breakers rolled gently to shore in a mesmerizing rhythm. They found a spot away from the few family groups and Adam spread out a blanket, set down the cooler and opened a small folding chair for each of them.

"You've thought of it all," she said, smiling.

"I even ordered good weather." He tilted his face back to the sky and she watched for a moment as he soaked up the warm rays of the sun that beat down on them. Then he shrugged out of his shirt. She couldn't keep her gaze from lingering on his hard, flat chest and stomach and the surprising bulge of muscle in his arms. A line of dark hair spread across his breastbone and then headed south, swirling around his navel and disappearing beneath the waistband of the royal-blue swim trunks he wore.

When she met his eyes, he was smiling, a slow, warm smile that unfurled a ribbon of heat from her head to her toes. "Your turn," he said softly.

Her breath caught in her throat. Slowly, she unbuttoned the oversize shirt she'd paired with casual shorts.

She stepped out of the shorts without looking at him, then slipped the shirt off and laid it across the back of the chair he'd set up.

Adam made a sound deep in his throat. "You're beautiful," he said hoarsely.

"Thank you." Flustered, she turned to conventional courtesies to hide her pleasure at his words. Sinking down into the low chair he'd set up, she patted the second one he'd dropped on the sand beside it. "Come and sit."

She rummaged in her bag for her dark sunglasses, very conscious of the proximity of his nearly naked body. She'd never felt self-conscious in a bathing suit before, but today she had to stifle the urge to reach back for her shirt.

"Tell me about your new sister," she said, trying to distract herself.

"Lea?" He sounded startled. He dropped into the chair beside her. "What do you know about her?"

"Only what the press has printed." She smiled wryly. "And I imagine the real story is probably very different."

He nodded, his mouth set in a grim line. "Yeah, the media likes nothing better than to take an innocent situation and make up a good, juicy story to go along with it. Who cares if it's true or not? Who cares who it hurts?"

"You sound like that's a personal statement." And indeed, there had been some note in his voice that told her there was more to the story.

"It is."

"If you'd like to talk about it, I'm a good listener," she offered.

He sighed. "It was years ago. I had a study session

planned with a friend who was in one of my college classes. I stopped by her house to pick her up, but when she started to walk out of the house, she fainted. It turned out she had the flu."

"And?"

"I caught her before she hit the ground. Her family is very wealthy and often is a media target. That day there happened to be a photographer who got a juicy shot of me holding Karis. Unfortunately, her fiancé wasn't the most trusting man in the world and it very nearly ruined their relationship. Not a real big deal, but it still leaves a bad taste in my mouth. Making up stories about people without knowing any of the facts should be illegal."

"Have there been stories made up about your new sister?"

He nodded.

"I imagine her sudden appearance has been difficult for your family," she said carefully.

He shrugged. "Not difficult, exactly." He sighed, reaching across the small space between their chairs and twining his fingers with hers. "We were surprised, for sure. Dad had no idea Lea existed."

"I imagine it was a bit of a shock finding out that your father had feet of clay," she said, trying to empathize.

"We knew that before." His voice was matter-of-fact. "He wasn't much of a dad when we were growing up. His military career came first. After my mother died, he didn't have a clue about how to deal with five rowdy kids."

"I suppose I meant that it must have been a shock to find out he'd had an affair," she said.

"It was a bad set of circumstances." He shrugged. "It wasn't as if he set out to cheat on my mother. He suffered a head injury in Vietnam and lost his memory. A group of villagers took care of him and he got involved with Lea's mother but he was rescued without knowing she was pregnant. Then, before he could get back to her, her village was torched and he was told there were no survivors."

"Oh, how awful."

He nodded. "The Viet Cong didn't take kindly to anyone helping Americans. And," he added, "it wouldn't have been much easier if he *had* found out about the child. After all, he was married with several legitimate children already."

She winced. "I imagine that would have been difficult to explain to his wife."

He made a sound of agreement. "From everything I hear, my mother's position in Savannah society was very important to her. It wouldn't have gone over well, I can guarantee."

They were silent for a moment, then he spoke again.

"I'm glad, though, that we've found Lea. Found out about her."

"So you like her?"

He nodded. "Very much. She's really beginning to feel like a sister."

"That's how I feel about my friend Willi," she said.

"Willi." He repeated the name. "Please tell me that's short for something."

She laughed. "Guillemette. I think I told you before that she's French. She's an only daughter, nine years younger than any of her brothers, and she says we're sisters of the heart." She sobered. "Most of my best memories are of times I spent with Willi and her family."

"Most of mine are from times at my uncle Harold's house. After my mother died, my brothers and sister and I spent most of our school holidays there instead of at Crofthaven."

She felt a surge of empathy. Even though he'd grown up in the midst of a large family, it sounded very much as though Adam had missed the same basic sense of belonging she had.

"My children," she said, "are going to know they're loved. No, they're going to be *smothered* in love." Abruptly, she realized how passionate she sounded, and embarrassment flooded her. Scrambling out of her seat, she flung down her sunglasses and headed for the ocean. "I'm hot. I think I'll get wet."

"Wait for me." Adam was beside her in a minute. He caught her hand as they walked toward the water. "In case I haven't mentioned it," he said, "you look terrific in that bathing suit."

She smiled, relaxing a little as she recalled his earlier words. "I got the impression you liked it," she said. "So do I. I just bought it when I moved here. Most of my old ones aren't legal in the United States."

"Wait," he said as she began to wade into the gently foaming breakers that rolled in to shore, "you mean you went topless?" He sounded mildly shocked.

"Well, yes. Everyone did."

"Yes, but I can't imagine you being comfortable—"

"When you're one relatively small set of breasts on

a vast beach of European women sporting implants, comfort level increases dramatically," she said, grinning. "No one was looking at me."

A wave larger than the rest surged past them and they both had to jump to avoid going under. Adam turned and did a lazy sidestroke around her. "I can't imagine you went unnoticed." He stopped and moved closer, catching her around the waist and tugging her gently toward him. "I'd notice you anywhere."

She put her hands on his shoulders, enjoying the flirtation. "You may be prejudiced." The drag of the water pushed her firmly against him and their legs tangled.

He drew her even closer. "Come here and let me kiss you and I'll show you just how prejudiced I am."

She laughed until his mouth covered hers. And then she gave herself to the sweet invasion, kissing him back, enjoying the slick feel of his skin sliding against hers beneath the water.

His leg slid between hers and she breathed out a moan as secret shocks of pleasure raced through her. Adam held her loosely, letting the water press her against him, then take her inches away again. He kissed her again and again as their bodies touched, parted and touched again, as she slid up and down his strong, muscled thigh and the hard press of his arousal flirted with the softness of her belly.

Finally, he set her away from him with a smile. "We'd better stop before we attract the wrong kind of attention," he said, touching her lips with a dripping finger. "This feels private out here but it's not. There's a whole beach full of people who think they know what we're doing right now.

Her eyes widened with shock at his blunt pronounce-ment. "Then we'd definitely better stop. Getting ar-rested wouldn't make either of our families very happy."

"It wouldn't make me happy, either, considering we weren't even doing what we'd be getting arrested for."

They grinned at each other for a moment, then she burst out laughing. "You," she said, propelling herself backward and swatting a sheet of water at him, "are a bad, bad man."

"Not half as bad as I'd like to be with you." The words were teasing but the look in his eyes was hot with promise. Then he tossed water back at her with one big hand and the sensual moment was over.

They played and swam for perhaps half an hour be-fore Adam pointed toward the shore. "Time to go in. You need more sunscreen."

She pressed a finger to her forearm, looking for signs of sunburn. "Thanks for reminding me."

They waded out of the surf and dried off, then for-sook the chairs to lie side by side on their stomachs on the big blanket he'd spread on the sand. She got them each a can of soda from the cooler and they let the warm September sun and the pleasant breeze take the excess moisture from their bodies.

Adam was quiet for so long that she thought he'd gone to sleep, but when she glanced over at him, she saw that his amber eyes held a faraway look.

"You're deep in thought." She smoothed a hand over his brow. "What are you thinking?"

To her surprise, his gaze shifted away from her. "Just…kicking around an idea."

This was important. She didn't know why, but she felt sure that whatever was going on in Adam's head right now was a key to understanding him. She propped her chin on her forearms and angled her head so she could see him better. "Sometimes it helps to talk an idea through."

Abruptly, his eyes focused on her again. He hesitated and she wondered what he was searching for as he gazed at her intently, almost as if he were trying to read her mind. "You can't laugh," he said.

She gave a small, unladylike snort that would have annoyed her father. "When have I ever laughed at you?"

He nodded once. Short and sharp. "I'm thinking about writing a book."

She was instantly intrigued. "A book about what?"

"A serious study of the ghosts and legends of the Savannah area."

"Sounds like an exciting project." She made no attempt to hide her interest. "What do you mean by 'a serious study'?"

A warm flare of gratitude and pleasure lit his eyes and the tension left his shoulders as he smiled at her. He propped himself on one elbow. "There are a number of books out there already about Savannah's ghosts," he said, warming to his theme as he apparently realized she was serious about her interest. "But most of them are simply a recounting of the more popular stories, with a little embellishment to titillate the tourists. I want to do more." He gestured with his free hand. "Which ones are simply legends and tall tales? Which ones might be exaggerations of something that occurred? Which ones are unexplained and persistent enough to be considered some kind of real psychic phenomena?"

"You've really given this some thought," she observed. "I think you should do it."

"Just like that?"

"Just like that." She nodded decisively. "I'd be happy to help with the research if you'd like a silent partner."

He was grinning, an exuberant, uncomplicated expression that made her smile in return. "You're amazing, do you know that? Most women run the other way when I start talking about Savannah history or ghosts." Then his smile faded as he looked into her eyes, and a deeper, warmer emotion lit the amber depths of his gaze. "Selene…we haven't known each other very long. But I've never met a woman like you. I've never seriously considered marriage and forever and kids before. I am now."

"Oh, Adam." She dropped her head against his shoulder, rolling on her side to hold him close for one dangerously hot, sweet moment. "You make me think about things like that, too. But until this election ends, I can't—we can't—"

"I know." He pressed a kiss to her temple. "I don't want to pressure you or make you uncomfortable. But I thought it was important to tell you how I feel."

"It's very important," she said. "*You're* very important."

Five

By unspoken agreement, they spent the rest of the afternoon on safer, less personal topics. The sun was warm and gulls wheeled and called overhead. In the background, the low, rhythmic roar of the waves was a soporific counterpoint to their conversation, and eventually, they dozed.

The stretch of beach emptied as the vacationers headed for their hotels to clean up for dinner and evening activities. Finally, they decided to pack up their things as well.

Folding the beach blanket he'd brought, Adam watched as Selene walked to the water's edge to rinse off the sand from her hands. She was long and lean, slender and yet definitely all woman, and the sight of her in the brief bikini she'd worn had kept his system at a low boil all afternoon. He felt like pinching himself as he recalled the feelings shining in her emerald eyes. Was it possible she could care for him as much as he was growing to care for her? He was almost afraid to consider that perhaps he'd found a woman with whom he could share his life. Sad as it was to admit, he'd almost given up on finding love.

Or maybe he hadn't really thought love existed. He couldn't even remember anymore why he'd thought he was in love with Angela. She'd been beautiful and attentive and he'd been young and dazzled. But he was positive he'd never seen the look in her eyes that he saw when Selene looked at him. And she'd certainly never tried to pretend more than cursory interest in anything he pursued. God, he could still practically taste the humiliation he'd felt when he'd overheard her with her best friend, laughing over his nonstop talk about the history of Savannah.

Honey, I just tune him out when he starts with that old-time stuff.

But, Ang, her girlfriend had said, *how can you stand it?*

The Danforths are loaded with a capital L. Believe me, I can stand a lot more than being married to a bore for that kind of money.

Selene started back toward him and he forgot all about the past, mesmerized by the gentle sway of her breasts and the play of muscle in her long, slim thighs. She hadn't known who he was when she'd met him. And while John Van Gelder might not fall into the same category of wealth that Adam's own family did, he certainly had more financial resources than the average

American. So even if he was concerned that she was after his money, which he hadn't considered at all after the first night, she would have no reason to need him in that way.

No, the soft smile she was aiming at him had nothing to do with money and everything to do with happiness. The same simple happiness he'd felt when he first caught sight of her. The kind that made his heart feel as if it were going to burst right out of his chest.

He wasn't ready for the day to end. And as she stopped at his side, he dropped the blanket and reached for her.

"Want to have dinner with me?" He had to stifle a groan of pleasure as her scantily clad body pressed flush against his.

"I'd love to." She stretched up to kiss his jaw. "I don't have anything on my schedule for this evening."

Regretfully, he set her away from him. Much as he'd like to continue holding her, a guy in swim trunks on a public beach had to exercise a little self-control. And his was fading in inverse proportion to the fit of his trunks. "All right. If you don't mind casual dining, the hotel right up there has an oceanside bar where we can order off the menu."

"That's fine." She tied a short skirt that matched her bikini around her hips. "Is this too casual? I can dress again if you like."

"No." He couldn't keep himself from grinning. "I think what you're wearing right now will do nicely."

She shook a finger at him. "You're so transparent."

He made a production of looking down at his trunks and acting scandalized. "I sure hope not.

That startled a genuine laugh out of her, and they gathered up their things and took them to the car.

"She's gone for hours at a time," John Van Gelder said to the burly man standing in front of his desk. "I want to know where my daughter goes and who she meets."

The man nodded. "Not a problem."

"She usually takes a taxi," the politician said, "and comes home in one as well."

"I can pick her up no matter what kind of ride she's got. You want pictures?" One beefy hand patted the camera hanging from a strap around the private investigator's neck.

"No! No pictures." Van Gelder studied the man. He wasn't altogether comfortable with this person, but the P.I. had been recommended by one of his constituents, so he probably was worrying for nothing. Just as he hoped he was worrying about Selene for nothing.

She'd been so quiet when she'd first come home. So compliant. But lately she'd been flitting out of the house for long periods with no real explanation and she seemed…distant. She'd always been eager to please as a child and he hadn't expected that to change. It worried him. What if she'd met some unscrupulous fellow who knew she was an heiress, if a modest one? What if she'd been seduced by some disreputable mongrel? There were a thousand unpleasant possibilities and he worried about every single one of them.

Selene was all he had, and although he suspected she thought he was as rotten a father as he believed he had been, he did care about his daughter. He closed his eyes briefly as an image of Elisabetta came to mind. Grief struck, sharp as it had been the day his beloved wife had died. Had it really been more than two decades since he'd last held her in his arms? Not a minute of his life had been worth living after she'd died. He had poured himself into work, into politics and campaigning, simply because it occupied his mind, kept him from thinking.

Until he saw Selene. His beautiful daughter so resembled the wife he'd lost that sometimes he barely could bring himself to look at her. It was an ignoble sentiment for a father, but there it was. Over the years, his life had been much easier to get through when Selene wasn't around to remind him of what he'd lost.

The recent months had been rough, but he needed her. And he was getting used to seeing that too-familiar face, almost looked forward to their usual breakfasts together. She'd grown into an astute, intelligent young woman. In any case, he needed Selene by his side, to counter that damned Danforth and his huge, seemingly perfect family that made for such great press. No matter what occurred with the Danforth tribe, Abe Danforth's campaign managed to spin it into pure gold. He wished he'd thought of hiring Nicola Granville before Abe had gotten to her—

"Mr. Van Gelder?" The gravelly voice brought him back to the present. "Anything else you want?"

"No," he said curtly, tossing an envelope containing the P.I.'s retainer across his desk toward the man. "Just go do your job. And get back to me as soon as you have information."

* * *

Adam knew he should take her home after dinner. Or to a busy corner where she could catch a cab, since he knew Selene would never consent to him driving her home. But he didn't want the day to end.

"Would you like to see where I live?" he asked as they drove back toward the city after a leisurely meal.

She hesitated for a moment. "I really shouldn't. I've been gone a long time."

"You didn't have any plans for this evening, did you?"

"No," she admitted. "My father was having a campaign strategy meeting over dinner, so he didn't need me. I imagine that will drag on for hours. They usually do."

"Then you have plenty of time for a visit," he said, ignoring the hesitancy in her tone. Every time the campaign came up between them, she seemed to withdraw from him. He reached across the seat and laid his hand over hers, squeezing gently. "I'm not ready to let you go yet."

"All right." She turned her hand up and he felt the tension drain from her as she let him link their fingers. "I'd like to see your home. But I can't stay long."

Euphoria rose within him and he had to tamp down the urge to yell, "Yes!" Raising her hand to his lips, he kissed the back of her fingers lightly. "Terrific."

When he pulled into a parking space in front of his home on West Gordon Street, Selene laughed aloud. "I suppose it would be very silly of me to imagine you living anywhere but here in the heart of the history of Savannah."

He felt a little sheepish. "I like the area," he said. "And it's not far from my main office, which is pretty handy."

"This is a lovely building," she said as he came around and opened her door. She swung her legs out of the car and stood, still wearing the bikini top and little skirt she'd had on at dinner, and he took her hand.

"I don't live in the whole thing, although I own all of it," he said. "It was a single-family home at one time, but in the late 1960s it was divided into two apartments. I have the main floor and there's a tenant upstairs."

"How long have you lived here?"

"Since I graduated from college and went into business with my cousin." He led her through the wrought-iron gate. "A couple of blocks that way," he said, gesturing, "is Mercer House. A best-selling book was set there and they made a movie from it. A lot of the scenes from the movie were actually filmed there."

"There are so many beautiful homes here," she said, glancing up and down the street. "Have many of them been broken up like yours?"

"A lot," he said. "There are some beautifully restored old town houses two blocks over on Jones Street. There also are a lot of bed-and-breakfasts and inns. These old properties are astronomically expensive to maintain and there just aren't that many people willing to pour a fortune into them."

"What a shame," she said softly. "I understand, of course, and I think it's wonderful that even in an altered state they still retain the historical ambience. But what a shame that things couldn't simply stay the way they were. It's much the same in Europe. Most of the old castles and historic buildings are either museums or tourist accommodations because the families simply can't afford the upkeep."

He nodded as he escorted her up the steps to the wide front door. "That's exactly what happened with this house, only it has an even more interesting tale. It was designed and built in 1819 by a famous Savannah architect named William Jay. Fortunately, it was located far enough south to survive the fire of 1820, which destroyed over four hundred homes closer to the waterfront. The original owner died in a yellow fever epidemic the following year and it was sold, but the family lost it after the Civil War when Sherman—" Suddenly, he realized he'd assumed a lecturing tone. "I'm sorry," he said ruefully.

"For what?" She tore her gaze away from the beautiful rose brick and white columns of the stately architecture and looked blankly at him.

"For, ah, boring you," he said. "I forget—"

"You forget that this could never bore me," she said firmly. "Tell me the rest."

He was silent for a moment. "I owe you an apology. I keep comparing you with other woman I've known."

"You must know a lot of the wrong type of woman." She smiled and laid her hand on his arm. "There are just as many who appreciate the history and cultural heritage of an area. Now please, finish telling me about your home."

"There was another fire in 1889," he said, "and that one came within a block of the house, but the owners and their servants stood outside with wet rags and beat out the sparks. They even got up on the roof and kept the embers from starting a fire. That family had the house the longest. In 1918, their only son was killed in World War I and the house was eventually left to a great-nephew, who lost it in the Crash of '29. It's been sold and resold several more times since then. The man who owned it before me is the one who split it up."

"How hard would it be to restore it?"

"I don't think it would be too difficult. He didn't change anything significant except add a few nonload-bearing walls that could be knocked down again."

"It would be an extraordinary project to restore the place, wouldn't it?" She made a sound of pure pleasure as he showed her into the grand entrance hall, comfortably cooled by the central air conditioning he'd installed. "Oh, Adam, this is lovely."

"The paint color is an original Savannah shade called 'Peach Leather Tint,'" he told her. "If I ever do restore it, I want to combine period furnishings and fabric designs with modern conveniences so that it reflects both the past and the present."

She laughed. "You're amazing," she said. "You should do it."

He shrugged. "I never had anyone to share my interest before."

"And now?"

"Now," he said, "I am constantly amazed that I haven't bored you to tears babbling on about Savannah history."

"You could never bore me," she said softly. She turned and smiled at him with the same warm glow in her eyes that he saw every time they shared an intimate moment. His body responded to the look, reminding him forcefully that he was alone in his house with a very desirable woman wearing very few clothes. Selene lifted a hand to his cheek and touched him gently with a single finger, and his blood heated. And then he saw her shiver.

"I'm sorry," he said. "I'm not being much of a host. Would you like to clean up and put on some dry clothes? I have a guest suite you can use."

He took her down the hallway to the guest room he'd restored. It had a private bath and he laid out towels and one of his bathrobes for her before forcing himself to walk toward the door. "I'm going to catch a quick shower, too," he said. "Just come out to the living room when you're finished."

He was in and out of the shower in ten minutes, and he caught himself pacing the living room after five more. He glanced at his watch. He estimated he had three-quarters of an hour or so before she showed up—

"You have a lot of books," Selene said as she appeared in the doorway.

He spun around. "Wow," he said at last. "I've never known a woman who could shower that fast."

She pretended to glare at him. "That's an extremely sexist remark."

"It also was a compliment," he said, grinning. He eyed her appreciatively.

She wore his bathrobe belted around her slim figure; the sleeves draped well past the ends of her fingers. Her hair was wrapped in a large white towel, and still she looked hauntingly lovely. "I glanced into your library," she said, apparently unaware of his thoughts. "Do you have a favorite genre?"

He shrugged. It was hard to concentrate on what she was saying when he was all too aware that with one tug on the belt of that robe, he could have it open, have her soft, lovely flesh in his hands, put his mouth on the warm slope of her breast—

"Tell me about your reading habits." She smiled when his gaze met hers and there was no flirtation in the look. But as their eye contact held, he saw the moment when she became aware of his interest. Her eyes grew heavy-lidded and a small, secret smile curved her lips.

He cleared his throat, determined to stop ogling her like a horny adolescent. "I'll do better than that. I'll show you. Would you like a drink first?"

He opened a bottle of wine and they carried it to the library, where they discussed his book collection. He showed her the extensive trove of volumes on local history and was amused when she took the towel out of her hair, and sat right down on the carpet with one of his favorites, a compilation of Savannah's history that included some of the earliest and most stunning photographs ever taken of the city.

"You can borrow that," he offered, sitting down beside her when she showed signs of forgetting his presence altogether.

"Oh! Forgive me." She laughed, slamming the book shut. "Willi used to get so mad when she tried to talk to me while I was reading. She says I'm hopeless."

Her face was lit with laughter, her striking eyes glowing emerald in the setting rays of sun slanting through the window. She was seated with her long legs tucked to the side and she lifted a hand, tucking her hair behind one ear as she chuckled.

Adam felt something tighten in his chest, a warm fist of need and desire that shocked him with its intensity. He leaned forward and set his lips against her laughing mouth.

Selene's hands came up to grip his shoulders as she made a small, sexy sound that inflamed his desire even further. He leaned forward and slid an arm about her waist, pulling her into his lap. He parted her lips easily and invaded the sweet recesses of her mouth, and her body relaxed against him.

The promise implicit in her surrender sent a bolt of heat boiling through his blood. "Selene," he muttered. He gathered her closer, deepening the kiss as his hand slid up the length of her leg where the robe had fallen open. He skimmed lightly up her torso and burrowed beneath the terry cloth, flattening his hand against the warm, satiny skin below her throat, then sliding his hand down, seeking softer, richer treasures.

Heedless of the bra she wore, he cupped her breast in his palm, seeing in his mind's eye the firm flesh of her body in the scanty bikini she'd worn. Lightly, he let his thumb graze her nipple. She moaned and arched her back, pushing herself against his hand, and he repeated the motion again and again until she was twisting and writhing in his lap.

Her movements pressed her hip against him, and he rolled to one side, laying her on the carpet and leaning over her as he kissed her, his hand still at her breast. He threw one leg over hers, bringing the throbbing length of his arousal directly against her hip, and the breath whooshed out of his lungs when she turned and arched against him, pressing her soft belly directly against the hard ridge behind his shorts.

He groaned, a harsh sound that echoed in the room as he yanked the fabric of the robe out of his way, baring her lacy bra to his avid gaze. "I want you," he said hoarsely.

Her cheeks were pink and her long lashes swept down to hide her eyes from his gaze, but she didn't tell him no. He could see that her bra clasped in the front, and he lifted his hand, twisting his big fingers until it popped open with a snap. Almost reverently, he lifted the lacy covering away, revealing her breasts, and she was so pretty, so perfect, that he almost stopped breathing. Her breasts were round and generous, the flesh paler where her bathing suit shielded her from the sun. They were crested by tight little points of rosy pink, and when he bent and took one taut peak into his mouth, she gave a strangled cry as her hand came up to press his head even closer to her.

He suckled her lightly, then paused to flick his tongue back and forth, blowing on her until her fingers tightened in his hair, pulling him back for a deeper taste again. He was only too happy to oblige, drawing her into his mouth with a strong suction and lightly scraping his teeth over the little pebbled point as her hips wriggled and pushed against him, shortening his breath with every motion.

He tugged impatiently at the belt of the robe until he'd pulled the garment completely apart and her soft belly was bared to him. Then his hand went to the fastening of his own pants. He felt frantic, wild for her, his body begging for direct contact. He couldn't open his zipper without fumbling, couldn't free himself fast enough. And at last, when he finally shoved his briefs out of the way and brought his rigid, straining length against the soft warmth of her belly, the sensation was so exquisite he heaved a sigh of relief that was almost a groan.

For a long moment, he simply held her there, clamped tightly to him with his erection firmly sandwiched between them.

She squirmed against him a little and his breath caught on a rush of ecstasy. "You feel so good," he said hoarsely.

"So do you." Her voice was little more than a whisper. He felt her hand slide down his side and palm his buttock.

"Touch me," he said, drawing back a little. He tugged at her wrist until she let him draw her hand between their bodies. "Feel what you do to me." She was still for a long moment, her hand unmoving in his. Then, slowly, her fingers uncurled and he shuddered as he felt her reaching out. As she touched him, his breath literally stopped.

And then she was exploring him with a light, tentative touch that brought the blood rushing to his head and tripled his heart rate as he fought to control his response. He let her explore, let her brush the length of him and forced himself to stillness even when her hand drifted lower to cup the sensitive flesh there. Finally, he couldn't take it anymore. He reached down and wrapped his fingers around hers, guiding her into a grip and rhythm that pleased him, groaning aloud when she eagerly picked up the motions on her own. An electric sizzle shivered down his spine and abruptly he grabbed her wrist before he came apart right there in her hand.

"Sweetheart," he said, even as his hips involuntarily arched forward, thrusting against her hip, "you have to stop that."

She withdrew her hand immediately and as he looked at her lowered eyelids, he realized she was embarrassed. "I didn't mean you're doing anything wrong," he elaborated. "But I want you so badly that I don't trust myself to be able to hang on to my control." He lifted a hand and tipped her chin up with one finger until she looked at him. "I want this to be perfect for you, too," he said.

"Oh." Her voice was faint. She cleared her throat. "That's not very likely, actually. I·haven't, ah, haven't done this before."

It took a moment for the meaning of her prim words to register. "You haven't…?"

She shook her head. "No."

He was stunned. He blurted out the first thing that crossed his mind. "We can't do this." Agitated beyond measure, he haphazardly pulled his robe around her before rolling away and rising, keeping his back to her as he tugged his briefs over his aching flesh and fastening his pants with difficulty.

"Adam?" Her voice sounded hesitant, unsure.

"Get up," he said. He knew his voice sounded harsh

but he was waging an internal battle that demanded all his willpower. Half of him, the noble, courteous half, told him he couldn't take her virginity, especially in a rushed act on the floor of his library. The other half was wildly aroused by the thought that she was willing to give herself to him, that she thought he was special enough to share such a gift—and that part wasn't easily dissuaded from finishing what they'd started.

He heard a rustle as she got to her feet unassisted and remorse shot through him. Relief, too. If she was upright, his nobler instincts were much more likely to triumph than if she'd continued to lie there waiting for him.

Then he heard another sound. A sniff. "I'd better go," she said in a subdued tone. Alarm shot through him and he whipped around.

"Wait!" he said, rushing across the room. She was nearly at the door and he grabbed her arm, swinging her to face him. She wouldn't meet his eyes but a tear escaped even as he watched, trickling down over the smooth peach of her complexion. "Oh, baby," he said, "don't. I didn't mean to hurt your feelings."

"It's all right," she said, drawing in a deep breath that made her chest rise and fall and nearly shot his good intentions to hell. "I understand."

"No," he said firmly. "You do not." He drew her to him, ignoring the resistance that stiffened her limbs, and slid his arms around her. "Virginity is a very special thing," he told her bent head. "I'm honored that you want me to be the man you share this moment with, but it isn't something that should be rushed, or made light of."

Her head came up and she eyed him cautiously. "I thought…I thought you didn't want me anymore," she whispered.

An incredulous laugh exploded from him. "Selene," he said, drawing her flush against him until she couldn't possibly miss the proof of his desire for her, "does this feel like a man who doesn't want you?"

She sniffed and smiled, shaking her head. "No," she said. Her gaze grew mischievous and she slowly rubbed herself back and forth over him until he closed his eyes and groaned softly in frustration.

"You're making me crazy," he said. He put a hand beneath her thigh and lifted one leg until she caught on and wrapped it around his hip. The position opened her intimately to him, and he tugged the robe out of the way until all that separated them were a few layers of fabric. Her panties were small and satiny and already wet when he slipped an exploratory thumb over the sensitive flesh between her legs.

Selene shuddered and her head fell back as if it were too heavy for the fragile stalk of her slender neck. "I thought you didn't want to do this."

"Now," he clarified, dropping his head and nuzzling the side of her neck as he reluctantly withdrew his hand. "We're not doing this *now*. I never said I don't want you. But if I'm going to make love to you for the first time in your life, I'm going to do it with plenty of time to get it right."

Before he could make a liar of himself, he forced his

hands away from the temptations of her body and set her from him, fisting his hands in the lapels of the robe and holding it closed. "Go get dressed. I'm taking you home before I change my mind and keep you here all night."

Selene lifted her hands and placed them over his, and when she raised her eyes to his he read indecision, need and more in their emerald depths. "You have no idea how badly I wish that were possible," she said softly. Then she lifted herself on tiptoe and kissed his cheek.

As she turned and left the room, he let the fabric of the robe slide slowly through his fingers until she was gone and he stood alone. There weren't even two months left until this election, he told himself. Then they could be together as much as they wanted.

You could marry her, said a little voice in his head. He bent and picked up the book he had told her she could borrow, but his mind wasn't on what he was doing.

"I just might," he said aloud, slowly. "I just might do that."

Six

Adam left a message on her voice mail the next morning, telling her he'd like to have dinner with her that evening. Selene called him back on his office line the moment her father left the house for a brunch appointment. When his smooth, deep voice answered "Hello?", she swallowed through a throat suddenly so dry she wouldn't have been able to spit if she'd needed to.

"A-Adam?"

"Selene." His voice dropped to an even lower register, growing husky and intimate. "I miss you."

"I miss you, too," she said honestly.

"Can you make dinner tonight? We need to talk."

"We talked all day yesterday," she said automatically.

"Not *all* day," he said, and she could hear the humor in his tone.

She blushed, even though he couldn't see her. Thank God. "I'm not sure I can get away tonight," she said regretfully. "Father might get suspicious. I've hardly been home lately." Not that he would miss her presence at the dinner table. On the rare occasions that they ate at home together, he usually had the television on and his eyes glued to the news.

"All right," he said. "I didn't want to do this over the phone, but…I've been thinking about what you told me last night."

She knew, from the tone of his voice, he meant about her lack of experience. "Yes?" she managed. "Thinking what?"

"Your first time," he said, "should be special. Do you trust me to make it special for you?"

"Of course." She didn't even have to think about it. "I would trust you with anything."

She could hear the smile in his voice when he said. "Good. Can you find a way to get away for the night on Friday evening?"

"You mean…all night?"

"All night," he confirmed. "We're going to take our time, not rush anything." He paused. "I want to wake up with you in a bed in the morning."

Her body tightened with anticipation even as her heart melted. "I'd like that," she whispered.

"So can you get away?"

She thought about it. "I don't see why not. But I can't go far."

"I'm going to take you further than you've ever been before," he promised her, and once again she felt a hot blush wash over her from head to toe. He chuckled. "Nothing to say?"

She cleared her throat. "Not on the phone."

He laughed even harder. But his voice dropped to a rough whisper when he spoke. "I can't wait to get you in my arms again."

"I can't wait to be in your arms again," she told him. "Where shall we meet?"

He gave her the address of a restaurant in the Historic District. "I'll meet you outside and we'll stow your bag in the car before dinner. I'm going to make reservations at a restored inn close by and we'll go there after dinner."

"We're not going to your house?" she asked, startled.

"No. This is going to be special. I'm hoping my home will be your home one day and that wouldn't exactly make it memorable, would it?"

Silence fell.

Had he really said what she thought he'd said? Meant what she thought he'd meant? "Adam—"

"Selene—"

They both spoke at the same moment.

"You first," she said promptly.

"All right." He spoke slowly, as if he were thinking about what to say. "I apologize for rushing you. I know you don't want to have lengthy discussions about the future until the campaign ends."

"I may have changed my mind," she said faintly. Was he thinking of *marriage?*

He chuckled again, and the intensity of the moment lightened. "If you mean that, we'll talk on Friday night. Among other things."

The sensual intent was back in his tone and her pulse hammered with excitement. "Friday night," she said. "Is that a promise?"

"I promise," he said. "We're both going to remember Friday evening for a long, long time."

Adam fumbled the phone back onto the cradle absently, imagining the blush that he was sure had crept into Selene's cheeks. Did she blush like that all over? *Soon,* he told himself. *Soon you'll know.* It was amazing that just the sound of her voice could make him feel so stupidly happy.

A knock on his office door interrupted his reverie. "Come in."

"Hey." His brother Ian stepped into the room, closing the door behind him. He stopped halfway across the room, eyeing Adam speculatively. "What's that sappy expression mean?" His hazel eyes sharpened. "You've met someone!"

Adam shot him a wry look. "Is it that obvious?"

Ian laughed. "To those of us who've been there, yes." He settled into one of the chairs opposite Adam's desk, crossing one leg over the other. "Spill it."

Adam shrugged. "Yes, I've met someone." He hesitated. "I think I love her."

Ian's eyebrows rose. "Whoa. This is fast."

"How long did you know Katie before you realized she was the one?"

His brother grinned. "Good point." He studied Adam speculatively. "You trust her?"

Ian knew how badly Adam had been hurt by Angela's callous attitude all those years ago. "I do." He sought for words to explain. "She's different. She's interested in the things I am. She likes talking about history and ghosts. She likes my home. She doesn't need to be escorted to the most exclusive party in town every night."

"Do I know this lady who's captured your affections?"

Adam hesitated. God, he wanted so badly to talk about Selene, to share the perfect woman he'd met with everyone he knew! "You know her family," he hedged.

Ian's brows drew together. "Why do I think there's a problem in that statement somewhere?"

"Because there is." Adam couldn't contain himself anymore. "Her name is Selene Van Gelder."

Ian's eyes snapped wide. "*John's* daughter? The one who just came back from Europe a couple of months ago?" When Adam nodded, he whistled. "Man, do you know how to find trouble."

Adam's lips curved ruefully. "It could be easier."

"But you think she's 'the one'?"

"I *know* she's the one," Adam corrected. "I've known it since the night we met."

"Which was when? And where? I wouldn't have thought it likely that you two would be running in the same social circles. Her old man thinks running for office is a blood sport."

"She was at the Twin Oaks fund-raiser near the end of July."

Ian's brow wrinkled. "At a Danforth campaign fund-raiser? That's weird."

Adam nodded. For the first time since the night they'd

met, he wondered what she had been doing at a fund-raiser for her father's opponent. Everyone knew John Van Gelder despised Abe Danforth way out of proportion to the elected office they both were hoping to win. "Yeah," he said, "but she didn't stay long. And it wasn't until a few weeks ago that she'd consider going out with me."

"So all this has happened in a matter of weeks."

"You didn't know Katie any longer than that." Adam felt unaccountably defensive.

"No, I didn't," Ian admitted. "But her last name wasn't Van Gelder, either." He hesitated. "So you're pretty serious about Selene?"

Adam nodded. "I was thinking of asking her to marry me." At the look on Ian's face, he quickly added, "Oh, she won't even introduce me to her father until after this campaign is over, so if she says yes, it'll be just between us for a while."

"I don't know whether to wish you luck or tell you you're insane," Ian said wryly. "But good luck, anyway."

Adam's office assistant buzzed him, and he held up a hand to his brother. "Excuse me for a sec."

"Jake's on line two," the young man said. "He says there's a management problem at D&D's in Atlanta."

Ian stood. "I'll get out of your hair." He turned, then looked back over his shoulder. "Good luck with your girl."

"Wait," Adam said. "What did you come in here for?"

Ian waved a hand dismissively. "Nothing major. I'll catch you later."

Adam picked up the phone, but his attention was still on his eldest sibling as the door closed. He couldn't shake the feeling that Ian had been going to tell him something important, and he wished he'd been more attentive. He knew Ian was still having trouble with their coffee bean suppliers—was there something more he hadn't told Adam?

By the time the taxi arrived to take her to the restaurant where she was meeting Adam on Friday evening, Selene was a nervous wreck. While her father had been preoccupied with the headlines yesterday morning, she had casually mentioned that she would be going away. As she'd anticipated, he'd barely acknowledged her. Surprisingly, his coolness didn't wound her as it once had.

Maybe that was because of Adam, she thought. Now that she had him, her father's approval didn't seem so important anymore. Had she simply been looking for love all these years?

Love. Oh, she had to admit it. She loved Adam Danforth. As unsuitable as his name would make him to her father, it was too late to turn back, to stop the feelings from growing into an entire body-filling feeling that made her so happy she almost thought her skin wasn't strong enough to contain it. She loved him. But she couldn't tell him yet. It wouldn't be fair until after the election.

As she was heading out the door with her overnight bag, a voice behind her demanded, "Where are you going?"

Selene jumped and turned around. "I told you, Father," she said in the calmest voice she could manage. "I was invited to spend the night with a friend." She couldn't quite meet her father's eyes, and her chest felt as if there was a hundred-pound weight resting directly on it. Had he somehow guessed what she was doing? She stifled an urge to laugh hysterically as she realized that if he knew *who* she planned to do it with, he'd be locking her in her room this very minute.

"Hunh." Her father made a dismissive gesture with one hand. "I forgot. Have a good time."

"I will." *Understatement of the decade!* She turned and slipped through the door before he could say anything else to her, before he could read the guilt on her face.

John Van Gelder watched his daughter climb into the taxi to meet her girlfriend, his face taut with displeasure as he realized he'd forgotten to ask her about her schedule for next week. He hadn't even gotten the friend's name, so he couldn't call her. And she probably had her cell phone with her, but without her planner, which was probably on her desk, he doubted she'd be able to answer him definitely. Besides, he knew from experience that she didn't have the phone turned on much of the time, anyway.

Oh, well, no matter. He could ask her tomorrow. Still, it irritated him that now he wouldn't be able to confirm his plans to have her attend several campaign events until she returned. Perhaps he should take a look at her calendar. Leave her a note asking her to reserve the dates he had in mind. Turning, he headed for the wide staircase.

A few moments later, he entered the small sitting room attached to his daughter's bedroom. Her delicate writing desk stood before one light-flooded window, computer and planner in plain view. He crossed the room and sank into the chair before the desk, but before he could check the dates in question, a beautiful coffee table book laid to one side caught his eye.

He drew the tome to him, idly flipping through the pages of extraordinary photographs of Savannah history. Very nice. He wondered where she'd gotten it. He wasn't big on history and was sure he had nothing like this. Selene always had been an odd child. For all he knew, she could be collecting things like this book now.

But as he closed the book, something written on the flyleaf inside the front cover caught his eye. Opening the book again, he read the handwritten signature and a muscle began to twitch in his jaw.

Adam Danforth.

Adam Danforth! What in hell was his daughter doing with a book that belonged to one of Abe Danforth's sons? As far as he knew, she had never even met them. He scoured his memory, but couldn't come up with a single time when Selene would have been introduced to any of the Danforth family. Even when he'd sent her to that ball at Twin Oaks a couple of months ago, she'd come home early saying she hadn't seen or heard anything interesting.

Maybe it was an accident that she'd acquired a book that had belonged to Adam Danforth. A coincidence. But still…he hadn't gotten to this point in his career by being careless.

Wheeling, he stalked into his office and rapidly punched in a number. When the line was picked up on the other end, he said, "I have a new assignment for you.

Adam Danforth. Find out everything about him and get back to me as soon as you can."

Adam was waiting for the taxi in front of the restaurant, and he helped her out, then leaned forward and gave her a brief but possessive kiss that nearly melted the shoes right off her feet. Then he tipped the cabbie and lifted her small bag. "Just let me put this in my car, then we'll go inside."

"Adam?" She clutched at his hand as he began to lead her toward the car parked nearby. "Do we…" She gathered her courage and began again. "We don't have to eat."

He stopped in his tracks. His eyes searched her face slowly. "You haven't had dinner."

"I'm not hungry," she said. *Except for you.* "We could eat…after."

Something moved deep in his eyes, something that sent a flash of heat through her body. "Are you sure?"

She nodded, smiling tremulously. "Oh, yes."

He smiled then, too. "All right," he said. He led her around to the passenger side of the car and helped her in. Once he was behind the wheel, it seemed a very short drive, only a couple of blocks, really, until he pulled into a parking space in front of a lovely old building that a discreet sign proclaimed was an historic inn.

He retrieved her bag and led her inside, holding her hand in his, and she wondered if he could feel her fingers trembling. She was trembling all over, or at least it felt like it, with anticipation, excitement and probably more than a few nerves as well.

Apparently he had registered before she arrived and

he took her straight to the lift that led to a room on the second floor. The hallway was hushed and cool and there was a stateliness about the old house that made her feel as if she should speak in whispers.

When he fit the key into the lock and ushered her into the room they would share tonight, she was charmed by the beautiful four-poster bed with its pineapple motif. The ceilings were high and there was a fireplace along the far wall. Two floor-to-ceiling windows were covered by lavish fabric and opposite the bed French doors led out onto a small, elegant balcony that overlooked a private garden. Tall trees at its far end gave the illusion of total privacy, since all view of other buildings was blocked by the canopy of branches.

"This is lovely," she said, taking in the small table on which stood a silver compote piled high with fresh fruit.

"Yes," he said, "it is."

But when their eyes met, he was looking at her rather than the room. He smiled and held out his hand. "Come here."

She went to him, lifting her arms around his neck as he drew her close. He was big and hard and warm and she felt fragile, feminine in his arms. A sudden pang of apprehension shot through her at the thought of what was to come, and he must have seen it.

"Are you certain this is what you want?" His eyes were golden in the late-day light slanting across the floor.

She saw from the tension in his face what it cost him to ask the question. "Positive," she said quietly, forcing her silly female fears to the back of her mind. Adam had never been anything but gentle with her, she reminded herself. He would make it as easy as he possibly could. That thought led to another, which she voiced. "I want you to be my first." *My only.* She slipped a hand from his shoulder up to his strong jaw, tracing the firm line of his lips with a single finger. "Make love to me, Adam."

His eyes caught fire. "With pleasure," he murmured.

He drew her finger into his mouth and sucked lightly on the single digit, his tongue swirling a warm pattern around and around, and she felt herself breathing faster, a heavy ball of arousal settling deep in her abdomen. She smiled, her eyes closing in pleasure as she swayed toward him.

He released her finger. Slipping one large hand beneath her chin, he tilted her face up to his and took her mouth, giving her deep, drugging kisses to which she could only respond helplessly. Her hands gripped his broad shoulders. Her head fell back and she gasped for air as Adam slid his mouth down her throat.

Cradling her in one arm, she felt his free hand between them, stripping off his tie and working down the placket of his shirt. "We've got on too many clothes," he said softly against her skin.

Willingly, she lifted her hands to the buttons as he released her. He shucked out of his suitcoat and tossed it at a nearby chair, then pulled his shirt free of his trousers. As she opened the last button, he unfastened the cuffs and tossed it at the chair, then took hold of his V-necked undershirt and peeled that off, as well.

She'd seen him just two days before in bathing trunks, but here, he suddenly seemed much larger and much...barer than he had on the beach. Was barer even a word? His chest was a solid wall of muscle, lightly dusted with dark hair that eased down to a thin line and disappeared beneath the waistband of his pants. His flat male nipples were small copper circles studded with tiny points.

Adam caught one of her hands and lifted it to his chest, lightly brushing her fingertips over one tight tip. His eyes closed and he made an approving sound deep in his throat when she whisked her fingers over him again. "That feels good," he said in a husky whisper. Then he lifted his hands to the line of buttons that marched down the front of her strappy sundress. "Will it feel good to you, too?"

She couldn't speak, could only stand on trembling legs before him as he unfastened her dress until it hung loosely, exposing a thin strip of flesh down just past her waist. She hadn't worn a bra because the dress had built-in cups, and when his fingers hooked beneath the straps and tugged them off her shoulders, the fabric separated abruptly, baring her breasts to his eyes.

"Sweet," he said hoarsely. He brushed the straps down until the dress caught at her hips, then gave it one last push so that it dropped around her ankles.

Selene felt herself blushing as she stood before him in nothing but a high-cut pair of lacy panties and the high-heeled sandals she still wore. Adam was breathing heavily, his gaze riveted to her breasts. "You're so beautiful," he whispered. He palmed her breasts almost reverently and her embarrassment faded as he cradled them, tenderly brushing his thumbs back and forth over the taut peaks he'd uncovered. The caresses shot streamers of fire licking through her system, zinging down to light a blaze between her legs where she felt herself soften for him. She shifted restlessly and saw him smile. "Yes," he said. "Do you want me?"

"Adam," she said, hearing the plea in the single word, and his smile widened as he bent his head and closed his lips over the tender tip of her breast. He suckled strongly, wringing a cry of pleasure from her as her knees went weak and she clutched at his smooth, bare shoulders. His arms came around her, pulling her hips firmly against him, and she gasped as she recognized the solid weight of his aroused flesh pressing hard into her soft belly. He still wore both his belt and his pants and the fabric of his trousers against her bare flesh was an erotic stimulant. The fire inside her was raging now, stoked by the incessant tugging of his mouth on her sensitive flesh, and she writhed against him, moving herself helplessly over his firm length.

Adam groaned. He released her and fumbled with his belt, tearing it open and unzipping his pants in the same motion. "Help me," he said, and his voice was little more than a growl, his eyes blazing with heat and need. Obediently, she put her hands in the waistband of his trousers and pushed them down. As they fell around his feet, she couldn't resist looking down at the white briefs he wore, stretched taut by the pressure of the very male flesh caught behind the elastic and fabric of the briefs.

Adam hooked a finger in the briefs and pulled them away and down and she swallowed at her first full sight of him completely unclothed, jutting forward proudly from the thicket of dark curls at his groin. She helped him tug the briefs over his hard buttocks, and then all his clothes were gone. Breathing as harshly as if he'd just run a mile, Adam set his hands at her waist and lifted her, stepping forward to free them both from the tangle of clothing on the floor, and as he drew her against him, she gloried in the satiny feel of his rock-hard flesh prodding at her soft belly. She curled her arms around his neck and her bare breasts were crushed against the hard planes of his chest, the springy hair teasing her nipples. He thrust his hips forward and she practically purred with pleasure. This was what she had been born for, this moment, this man. Slowly, she moved her hips against his, her breasts sliding over his chest.

He took her mouth again and she felt his hand on her thigh, urging one leg up and holding it wrapped around his waist as she had the other night. The position left her vulnerable, balanced on one slender high heel, and when he pulled her into firm contact with him, they both groaned. She still wore the small panties, and as she felt him rubbing himself steadily against the satiny fabric that barely covered her, she was astonished by the waves of pleasure lifting her higher and higher. Moaning, she angled herself against him to increase the wonderful sensation.

He swept her into his arms and carried her to the bed, setting her on her feet so that he could sweep the covers back. Then he placed her on the mattress and came down beside her, propping himself on one elbow as he looked down at her.

She looked up at him, eyes wide. She'd felt exposed when he'd first removed her clothing, but now, lying down, she felt much more vulnerable. Against her hip, she could feel the hard proof of his desire for her, twitching and moving occasionally.

Slowly, he lifted his hand and laid it flat on her belly and she sucked in a startled breath at the heat that leaped between them. "I want you," he said, "more than I have ever wanted anything in my life." He let his gaze slide down from her face over the rest of her body, and a slight smile touched his lips.

"Adam," she whispered, overwhelmed by the intensity of his tone, "kiss me."

The smile widened. "Gladly."

Leaning over her, he touched his lips to hers, lightly at first. Then, with more and more amorous intent, his mouth grew firmer. He touched the line of her lips with his tongue and when she opened to him, he immediately swept in to claim the sweet recess as his own. His free hand slipped up over her torso and found a breast, and he firmly rotated his palm over it as the temporarily banked fires he'd lit within her flared to life again. Her body arched and he chuckled. His hand left her breast and began to slowly journey down her body. At the same time, he slid his mouth from her lips along the line of her jaw until she felt his hot breath in her ear. She jumped as he drew her earlobe into his mouth and began to suckle, and her hips lifted involuntarily at the shocking sensations his mouth produced. Who would have thought an ear could be so erotic?

But the thought barely cleared her consciousness before it scattered again as his hand slowly traced firm circles down past her naval, each time slipping a little farther, making her shiver with anticipation.

Finally, he slipped a finger beneath the elastic edge of her panties. "These have to go," he said, making short work of them.

As he tossed them over his shoulder, she realized she was still wearing her shoes, and she said, "Let me take off—"

"No." He grinned, lifting one long slender leg and looking down the bare length of it. "I kind of like this look." Then his gaze traced a path back up over her body until he came to the newly exposed nest of soft curls that covered her. He combed his fingers through the curls, watching his hand as his fingers slipped down, curving between her legs. "And this look," he said hoarsely. "I *really* like this look."

He moved his fingers a little, and she jumped, squeaking as spears of pleasure shot through her body.

"Relax," he whispered, pressing against her inner thigh with the heel of one hand until she let him open her.

"I can't," she whispered back. "It feels…too good."

His eyebrows arched and she felt the fingers rubbing tiny circles, spreading the moisture that he'd found between her legs over his hand and her flesh, making the contact even more pleasurable. "You're so wet," he murmured. "Wet for me."

"Adam!" She clutched at his shoulders, uncaring that she was pleading. "Stop! I can't—I can't—"

"Yes, you can." There was a smile in his voice, but the tone was strained. "Let go, sweetheart. Just let go." He was crooning to her, low syllables of praise and encouragement, but she barely heard him. Her body was gathering tight, a taut fist of trembling need in her abdomen, her heels digging into the bed as she pushed herself against his hand, unable to resist the seduction of those knowing fingers.

He rose over her, still touching her as he lowered his head and took her breast into his mouth, and she cried aloud as sharp arrows of pleasure assaulted her. She couldn't stand it, and her needy, aching body rose again and again to the sweet lure of his magic fingers, drawing her tighter and tighter...

Until the delicious tension snapped and she screamed, arching against his hand. Waves of incredible pleasure swamped her, breaking over her head and she felt his hand between her legs, fingers plunging deep as she thrust herself against him over and over.

"Adam!" she cried out through the storm of sensual fulfillment.

"I'm right here." He bent and pressed a kiss to her forehead.

She was panting and winded, lethargy rushing through her to replace the wild excitement of moments ago. But the feel of his hard strength still pushing at her hip was a seduction all its own. She reached down and circled him, softly stroking the hot, smooth length of him, and incredibly, she felt a lingering echo of the intense pleasure she'd just known. "I want you right *here*," she said, spreading her legs wide and urging him to her.

He rolled atop her and she gasped with pleasure as he settled intimately against her. "Here?"

"Oh, yes. Please," she breathed. She moved a little, and he closed his eyes.

"Wait," he said. "We need protection."

He reared up on his knees and reached to the table at the side of the bed, and as he efficiently tore open the small package he must have placed there earlier, she was warmed by his care. As he rolled the condom into place, she reached out to help him, and with a groan, he thrust himself into her hands, letting her stroke and explore.

Finally, he came down onto her again. She wrapped her legs around his hips and held tightly to his shoulders as she felt him begin to sink into her. Closing her eyes, she waited for the pain.

Adam was slow and careful. She felt him hesitate when her body resisted—and then a single stroke pushed him deep inside her. Amazingly, there was almost no pain. The small pinching discomfort quickly faded and she opened her eyes to see his worried face above her. "Okay?" he asked.

She loved him even more for that. His arms were quivering and his whole body trembled with his need, and yet he was still concerned for her. "Perfect," she answered. She lifted and lowered her hips experimentally, enjoying the sensation of smooth full pressure that brought a return of the wild pleasure she'd already known.

And then Adam began to move. Long, powerful strokes that moved her body on the bed. Deep thrusts that ground her sensitive woman's flesh against his hard male length as their bodies came together again and again, wet flesh rubbing and slapping in erotic rhythms. He was breathing loudly in the quiet room and she suddenly realized that the small whimpering sounds of pleasure were coming from her own throat. In mere moments, the thrilling sensations hurled them over the edge into intense fulfillment simultaneously.

She dozed in the circle of Adam's arms but when he shifted, she blinked sleepily. "Sex must be like a drug," she said. "I'm exhausted and I didn't even do anything."

"That," he said, "is entirely a personal point of view." He grinned as she blushed, then glanced at the wristwatch he still wore. "It's almost nine o'clock. Are you hungry? We missed dinner, remember?"

"I remember." She considered the question as she lifted a hand and lightly traced a pattern across his breastbone. "No, I don't think I'm hungry. A piece of that fruit on the table would be fine for me."

"Good," he said with deep satisfaction, and she felt him stirring against her inner thigh where she'd laid one leg across him. His hand slipped down to her breast and she drew in a gasp of delight at the way her body immediately responded. "I can think of a lot of things I'd rather do than eat."

Seven

Adam woke slowly, filled with a deep happiness. The first thing he was aware of was that he wasn't alone. The second conscious thought was that Selene lay beside him, snuggled into a little ball while he curved possessively around her.

He opened his eyes and took in the warm light of day seeping around the edges of the curtains he'd closed last night. Glancing at the clock on the bedside table, he saw that it was just past seven. In a few short hours they would have to part.

Dissatisfaction rushed through him and he tightened his arms, drawing her closer. He didn't want to let her go. Not today, not ever.

The thought crystallized immediately. No, he didn't want to ever let her go. He loved her. He wanted to marry her. He wanted to wake up every morning with her in his arms, he wanted to see her belly swollen with his child. He wanted it all.

"Ummm." Selene stretched as she came awake, pushing her bottom back against him, and he forgot every thought in his head as he responded to the press of her soft flesh against his hips.

He slipped a hand up to her breast, idly flicking his thumb back and forth until he felt the tight little nubbin. "Good morning," he said into her ear as he kissed the side of her neck.

"Good morning." She reached behind her, wrapping one delicate hand around him and slowly sliding it up and down. "It feels like a *very* good morning." There was a smile in her voice.

"It surely does," he agreed. He could barely get the words out through the passion that clouded his brain as her fingers teased him.

He put one big hand on her thigh, lifting her upper leg and hooking it back over his, shoving himself forward into the warm, moist little nest between her legs but not entering her. "Are you sore?"

She turned her head so he could see her face, and she was smiling. "No."

"Good." He reached for protection and rolled it into place, then angled his hips and pulled her leg higher, opening her as he pushed deep into her. She was soft and wet and so warm he had to stop moving and grit his teeth in order to keep from ending their pleasure too soon.

And the next time he looked at the clock, nearly an

hour had passed. He was lying on his back this time, and Selene lay on his chest, her head against his heart.

"Are you awake?" he whispered.

"Mmm-hmm." She turned her head and kissed his chest.

"I think—" he said reflectively. "No, that's not right. I *know* that I love you."

Her head shot up and she propped herself on his chest, her mouth forming an *O* as shock widened her eyes. "Don't tell me that!"

To say that he was taken aback was an understatement. "Why not? It's true."

"It's too soon," she said, pushing herself upright. "Don't you think it's too soon, Adam? You barely know me."

He raised his eyebrows and slowly smiled. "I know you."

"I didn't mean *that*!"

"I know. It was just the perfect opportunity and I couldn't resist."

She shook her head, smiling now herself.

"And I think you're falling in love with me, too."

Her eyes softened. "Maybe I am," she said. "But we can't talk about this again until after the election."

Hurt began to create a dull ache around his heart. "You're willing to sleep with me, but I can't tell you I love you?"

"I'm willing to make love with you," she corrected, and he saw the now-predictable blush beginning to spread up her cheeks.

"Selene, you're not making a lot of sense." He tried

to keep smiling, though it was an effort. "I promised you that we wouldn't say anything to anyone about our relationship until after the election. But I am not going to promise not to say what I'm thinking."

"I'm afraid we'll jinx it," she said, still blushing. "Us, together—we're so wonderful, Adam, so perfect and amazing. Do you know what I mean? I guess I'm afraid that something will go wrong if we aren't careful."

"Sweetheart." He gathered her into his arms again, pulling her against the long, hard length of his body as the hurt receded. "Nothing is going to go wrong. We just have to be careful for a few more weeks, and then we can announce it to the world."

She sighed, angling her head to rest against his shoulder. "You don't know my father. It isn't going to matter if it's a day or a year after the election, and it isn't going to matter who won and who lost. All he'll see is that I'm crossing enemy lines."

"Crossing enemy lines," he repeated. It sounded ridiculous, but he'd seen some of Van Gelder's rabid attacks on his father, so maybe it wasn't so far-fetched.

"Thank you for last night," she said into the hollow of his throat. "It couldn't have been more special if I'd planned it all out."

"You're welcome." He gently ran his palms up and down her back, not feeling the need to say more.

"I do care for you," she said quietly. "More than I've ever cared for anyone. And once this campaign ends, I promise you we'll make plans. No matter what my father says."

"Good. I'll hold you to that." His voice was warm with satisfaction. "And we'll announce it to the media *before* they leak it, for once."

He let her have the shower first, sensing that she needed some private time. He had breakfast brought up while she finished in the bathroom, and after he'd taken a quick shower and dressed, they sat down to eat.

Afterward, they prepared to leave.

Adam glanced at her as he prepared to heft their bags, then abruptly reached for her, shocked to see tears filling her beautiful eyes. "Don't cry, baby," he said roughly. "It won't be long until we can be together as much as we like, remember? Just seven weeks."

"Just seven weeks," she repeated shakily.

"I promise," he said. "You know in your heart we have something special here. Something lasting."

She looked up at him then and smiled, though her lips trembled. "Yes," she said. "Something lasting."

He wiped the tears from her cheeks with his thumbs and kissed her forehead tenderly. Then slowly he stepped back and released her. "Are you ready to go home?"

She nodded.

Adam picked up her small bag and held the door open, and she preceded him into the hallway and down to the lobby. He glanced at her as he held the lobby door open. She was smiling rather sheepishly, her tears gone.

"What?" he said.

Her smile widened. "I feel like a wicked woman," she whispered. "Everyone's staring at us. I'm sure they know we never left our room once after we arrived."

Adam chuckled. "I think you're giving people credit

for being a lot less self-absorbed than most of them really are. I doubt anyone even could describe us." He steered her through the front door and began to lead her around to where he had parked.

"Wait," she said. "I'll take a cab."

"It's all right." He opened his trunk and set her bag inside. "I don't have anything big going on this morning. I have plenty of time to run you home."

She glared at him as he walked her around to the passenger side and opened her door. "It would be better for me to take a cab."

"No, it wouldn't," he said, calmly ignoring the fact that he *knew* she didn't want him to take her home.

She narrowed her eyes, but he was impervious. "All right," she said. "But only because it's the middle of the morning and I know my father won't be home."

He grinned, victorious.

And when they arrived in the big circle in front of her family home, he wouldn't let her out of the car until they'd made arrangements to have dinner again the following evening and she'd given him a very satisfactory farewell kiss.

"Why do you have a book that belongs to Adam Danforth?"

She was barely in the front door when her father popped out of his study and came toward her.

She froze, shocked that he was still at home in the middle of a weekday morning. Even more shocked at the chance she'd just taken. Had he seen Adam? She didn't think so or he wouldn't be half as calm as he was.

She focused on his question, schooling her face and voice to reveal nothing. There had been so few reasons in her life to practice lying that it never even occurred to her to try.

"I met him at that fund-raiser you made me attend," she said simply. Not a lie at all.

"I thought you said you didn't find out anything important there."

"I didn't. He isn't any more interested in campaigning than I am."

"But you did speak with him."

"He's a font of knowledge about Savannah history." Well, that was no lie, either. She took a deep breath. *You're a consenting adult,* she reminded herself. *You don't need his permission to do anything and he can't keep you from seeing Adam.* To her surprise, she couldn't prevent a slight sharpness from creeping into her tone when she spoke again. "This city is where my mother's family lived for generations, and yet I know next to nothing about it."

Her father looked completely taken aback. "Uh, I suppose we can fix that."

"I've already taken care of it myself," she said coolly. "And what were you doing snooping around in my suite?" She knew exactly where she'd left Adam's book. Not in a million years had she imagined her father would think to enter her rooms.

"I, uh, I wanted to check your schedule," he said, still staring at her as if he wasn't sure who she was. "I just wanted to leave you a note asking you to be available for some campaign activities this week and next."

"All right," she said. "I doubt I have any conflicts. I'll let you know." She swept past him and moved toward the stairs, out of patience with her father's odd behavior. "And good morning to you, too, Father." She colored her tone with the sarcasm he so often employed.

"Selene?" Behind her, his voice was strangely diffident.

She stopped with one hand on the newel post and turned to look back at him, eyebrows raised in inquiry.

"I…thank you for coming home," he finally said, gazing down at the thick rug on which he stood. "It means a lot to me."

"I understand that it's important to you to win this election," she said.

"No, that's not it." Her father lifted his gaze to hers and shock slapped at her. He looked as if…as if he were *fond* of her. "I'm just glad you're here. And I promise as soon as this election is over I will spend some time showing you the things your mother loved about this city."

Tears stung the backs of her eyes and she bit her lip. If he'd ever mentioned her mother before, she had no memory of it. "I'd like that," she said quietly. "I'd like that a lot." But as she turned and began to mount the stairs, she cautioned herself not to count on anything. If he won the election, he was going to be far too busy to bother with her. As usual.

And if he lost…she shook her head silently. If he lost, she couldn't imagine how he was going to react.

As she climbed the stairs to her room, her cell phone rang. Her heart gave a little leap of excitement and she realized she automatically assumed it was Adam, since very few other people had the number.

"Hello?"

"Hello, dearest!" It was Willi.

"Hi, Willi." Even though it wasn't Adam, it was the second-best thing. "How are you?"

"Utterly wonderful. But I want to hear about you! Last time we spoke, there was a lilt in your voice I've never heard before. Are you still seeing your Danvers fellow?"

"Danforth," Selene said in a near-whisper. She slipped into her suite, closed the door and crossed to her bedroom. Only when that door, too, was solidly closed behind her did she resume a normal tone. "His name is Adam Danforth."

"So you *are* still seeing him!" Guillemette's voice was triumphant.

"Yes."

"Selene! You sound as if things are going well."

"Things are going very well." She knew she sounded dreamy but she couldn't help it. "Adam says he loves me."

"Ohhh." Willi's sigh was nearly a coo. "Darling girl, that's wonderful. Are you making any plans I should know about?"

"Not yet." Selene sighed, the bubble of happiness leaking a little. "We don't want to do anything until after the election."

"The election that either his father or yours will lose?"

"Exactly."

Willi was silent for a moment. "How do you think it's going to go?"

"I have no idea. But if my father loses, telling him my boyfriend's last name is Danforth is going to send him through the roof. You'll probably see the fireworks in the sky from your side of the Atlantic."

Willi chuckled. "Surely not that bad. What's the very worst that could happen?"

"He could disown me, I suppose. Never speak to me again."

There was a loaded silence. Finally, Guillemette said, "Well, darling, I hate to point out the obvious but the man has ignored your existence for most of your life." There was a bite in her tone. Willi's family had strong opinions about the lonely little girl Willi had begun dragging home for boarding school holidays all those years ago. "I mean," she added, "you've lived without him quite well, and I daresay you could do so again."

"You're right." Selene sighed. "But you know, Willi, I feel sorry for him. He can barely mention my mother's name. Still, after all these years, he's grieving."

"And you know this because…?" Willi wasn't so quick to forgive the years of emotional neglect.

"He's been speaking of her a little bit. He says I look a lot like her."

Willi made a noise that possibly could be construed as sympathetic. "I can see how that would be difficult for him." She hesitated. "But, Selene, you aren't going to allow him to dictate whom you love, are you?"

"No." She had resolved that concern, and it showed in her voice. "Adam and I aren't going to let anything get in the way our relationship."

"Wonderful! I am going to have to start planning a trip to the States to meet this man. Or," she added slyly, "you could always bring him along to my wedding, get

married while you're here and take a long honeymoon
trip on the Continent."

Selene just smiled. "Perhaps."

"Has he asked you to marry him?" Selene had to
hold the phone away from her ear.

"No," she admitted. "He knows I couldn't accept right
now. And we haven't known each other very long—"

"Pah. Time means nothing when two people fall in
love."

From Willi's perspective, that probably was true.
She'd accepted a proposal after just four dates with her
husband-to-be. The fact that it had sent royalty across
half of Europe scrambling to be sure it was an accept-
able match had been of no consequence to either of
them. Selene felt cowardly and small by comparison.
Adam had met her more than halfway. Maybe he was
right. And so was Willi. If she wanted him, she needed
to show him that she didn't care about what the world
thought. Especially her father.

"Well, I can't tell you how to live your life." Willi
sighed dramatically. "Much as I want to."

Selene chuckled. "I appreciate your concern. You know
that. Now tell me why you *really* called. Have you made
a decision on the color of my maid of honor gown yet?"

Two days was a ridiculously long time to be separated from Selene, Adam decided the following day.
Why did her father dislike his family so much? And
why, given that he was pretty sure the man hadn't figured prominently in Selene's childhood, was she so determined not to upset him?

John Van Gelder might be a complete loser as a father, but he was all Selene had, Adam reminded himself. Selene hadn't had the love and support of other family members throughout the years of her father's neglect as he had. In her mind, even a loser was better than nothing. He could understand that.

His own father hadn't been around a lot when he was a kid. And while he saw his father's actions from a different perspective as an adult, there was still a little kid inside him who would never understand or forgive the benign neglect to which he'd been subjected. Thank God for Uncle Harold and Aunt Miranda. The "other" Danforth home had been filled with laughter and love and warmth and caring, and Abe's children had been as welcome there as Harold's own.

He was returning to the office from having lunch with Lea, when he stopped at the desk of his administrative assistant, Geoffrey.

"There's a lady to see you," the young man said. He grinned. "A fine-looking lady."

Adam lifted his head, alerted by something in the tone. "Did she leave her name?"

Geoffrey shook his head.

"Where is she?"

"I let her wait in your office. She has a book that belongs to you. When she showed me your signature on the flyleaf, I figured she was okay."

A book…Selene! He was shocked by the surge of pleasure that rushed through him. He practically bolted for his office door.

"Hey," he said as he entered the room and closed the

door firmly behind him. "What are you doing here?" He couldn't believe she'd been bold enough to come here. He knew how she worried about her father finding out about them.

"I wanted to return your book." She rose from the seat she'd taken at the small arrangement of chairs around an antique coffee table he'd found several years ago. His book lay on the table before her. "And maybe," she said, smiling, "I thought I could get a kiss or two to keep me going until tomorrow night."

He grinned, delighted at her unexpected appearance. "I think that could be arranged." He met her halfway across the room and put his hands at her waist, pulling her to him. "Hello," he murmured as he set his mouth on hers. But even as he sank into the embrace, his mind wouldn't shut off. "What about your father?" he murmured. "You're taking a huge risk coming down here."

She shrugged, framing his face with her small fingers. "You're worth a few risks." Her eyes were very green and determined, and he wondered what had occurred that had emboldened her so. She certainly couldn't be described as timid, but she worked hard to avoid controversy. If she had been recognized coming in here, things could get tense between her father and her in a hurry.

"Tomorrow night is too long to wait to see you," he said, cuddling her against his chest. "Let's get together tonight. We'll go out for dinner and then head back to my place."

"I can't," she said regretfully. "I need to stay at home this evening."

"Why?" He kissed her tenderly. "I don't want to wait until tomorrow evening, Selene."

"It's only a day," she teased him. Then her smile faded. "But I feel the same way. I shouldn't have stopped in here today but I wanted to see you." She paused, letting her hands slide up into his hair and he shivered as her fingers lightly traveled over his scalp. "I *needed* to see you."

"I'm glad." The tenderness faded from his expression, replaced by hungry desire. "I've been missing you, too."

He bent his head and found her mouth, kissing her deeply, sweeping his hands over her slender frame as his body sprang to full alert. She was like wildfire in his arms, twisting against him, igniting passion with every touch, every brush of her soft curves against him. He arched her backward, kissing her neck and sucking her earlobe into his mouth as he swirled his tongue over her satiny flesh. She shivered and clutched at his shoulders. As she lifted her arms, the short sweater she wore rode up her midriff and his seeking fingers encountered bare, creamy skin stretched over the delicate bones of her rib cage. He slid one hand up beneath the sweater, seeking her breast—

—And the door opened.

The sound was like the shock of cold water being thrown over his head. His head jerked up and he straightened, although he didn't let go of Selene, palming the back of her head and pushing her face into his shoulder to hide her identity.

His brother Marcus stood frozen just inside the door, his face a picture of amused surprise. "Well, hey. Guess there was a reason Geoffrey was trying so hard to head me off."

Adam's flustered assistant appeared in the doorway behind Marcus. He was practically wringing his hands. "I tried," he said to Adam, shaking his head in annoyance as he eyed Marcus. "I really did."

"It's all right, Geoff," Adam said. To his brother, he said, "Hello, Marc. I imagine there's a good reason for you to barge into my office."

His younger brother's grin was a rare sight. Marcus had always been driven, but after he'd caught his fiancée in bed with his best friend a year ago, his smiles had all but disappeared. "It can wait. Introduce me."

Adam heaved a sigh. "All right, but you have to promise not to tell anyone you met her until after the election."

Marc's brow furrowed. "After the election?"

"Selene, this is my idiot brother, Marcus Danforth. Marc, Selene Van Gelder." Gently, he set Selene away from him as she lifted her face from his shoulder and turned to greet his brother.

Instant comprehension lit Marcus's dark eyes. "Whoa." He offered Selene his hand. "Your father doesn't have much use for anyone named Danforth, I understand."

Selene shook her head ruefully as she took his hand. "No, I'm afraid not." She glanced up at Adam and smiled when he met her gaze. "But that isn't going to matter. We're only waiting until the election is over so that we don't distract either of our parents."

Marcus gave a short snort of unamused laughter. "You'd have to do a lot more than hang out with Adam to distract our father." He released her hand and backed toward the door. "I apologize for barging in."

"Wait," Adam said. "What did you want?"

But Marcus only shook his head. "Not important." Another of the rare smiles lit his sober features. "Carry on. Nice meeting you, Selene. I'll see you again when you two come out of hiding, I hope."

She smiled. "Most definitely. It was nice to meet you, Marcus."

As the door closed behind him, she turned to Adam, still smiling. "Now where were we?"

Eight

Adam didn't smile in return. It was as if his delight in her visit had vanished with his brother. "It's only September," he said. "Are we really going to have to hide our relationship for another month and a half until this damned election's over?"

She stilled at the grim note of frustration in his tone. "It would be best."

"Best for whom?" he demanded.

She'd never seen this side of him, this restless impatience, and it made her feel small and selfish. "Best for us," she said quietly, trying not to give way to her distress.

"It's not best for me." His tone was distinctly grumpy. "My father doesn't give one flying damn what any of his offspring do or who we date. Your father is the only one with the problem."

"I know." She was near tears. "But he's the only living relative I have, Adam, and I don't want to alienate him needlessly. All I'm asking for is seven weeks. Is that really so much?"

His expression softened, and to her relief he reached for her again, gathering her close. "No. Not compared to the rest of our lives."

The promise implicit in his words thrilled her. So he really was thinking of marriage!

He sighed. "It's just that I want to be with you all the time. I want to take you out to dinner or to a party and not have to worry about someone seeing us and tattling to some gossip columnist." His voice had risen again. There was a moment of tense silence and then she felt his taut muscles relax. "I want to introduce you to my family," he said in a more moderate tone. "I want the world to see us together."

"No more than I do," she told him softly, reaching up to cradle the strong line of his jaw. She understood now why it was so important to him; he'd been crucified in the media once and wasn't about to let it happen again. "I know seven weeks seems like a long time, but it will go quickly. I promise."

"Not quickly enough for me," he grumbled. But he bent his head and kissed her again and she realized the moment of discord had passed.

"Tomorrow night," she promised when he finally lifted his head. "I'll see you then."

"I don't guess you'd let me pick you up," he said, though it was clear he already knew the answer.

She shook her head. "Why don't I take a taxi to your place and we can go from there?"

He was watching from a window when Selene's taxi pulled up outside his gate the following evening. He opened the door and stood waiting as she came up the walk, marveling at the good fortune that had brought her his way. She walked with the fluid grace of a dancer, and he recalled how gracefully she'd matched his steps that first night in the garden, how perfectly her body had fit against his.

She came up the steps smiling quizzically. "Good evening. You look as if you're a million miles away."

He smiled, murmuring, "Not so very far." He stepped aside, holding the door wide for her, enjoying the slight brush of her body against his as she entered his home.

She stopped on the patterned rug in the foyer and laid her purse on the hall table beneath the wall-mounted mirror. For a moment, her back was to him, and the perfect curves of her heart-shaped bottom were beautifully outlined beneath the little skirt she wore. The pleasant arousal that had been simmering inside him since he'd first glimpsed her long legs uncoiling from the cab ratcheted up a notch and he stepped in close behind her. Setting his hands at her waist, he drew her back against him. He used his mouth to brush aside the hair at her neck and set his lips against the gently beating pulse he found there, kissing her lightly beneath her earlobe until she shivered and pressed herself back against him.

Adam groaned as he was sandwiched between their bodies, nestled between the sweet globes of her bottom.

He slipped his hands beneath the short sweater she wore and boldly palmed her breasts through the lacy bra she wore.

Selene made a small sound deep in her throat as he flicked his thumbs across the sensitive peaks until they were pebbled and hard, standing out even through the bra. Her small hands slid back to clutch his buttocks and pull him harder against her, and she gently rotated her hips, rubbing her bottom against him.

The world around him receded to one simple, over-whelming fact: he wanted her. Now.

Quickly, he slid his hands down her hips to the hem of the skirt and he tugged it up to her waist. To his delight, she wore a lacy black thong beneath it. Tracing his fingers gently along the scrap of fabric, he followed it down between her thighs. When he applied gentle pressure, she willingly widened her stance. He looked down her long slender legs and realized she still wore the small strappy heels in which she'd minced up his steps, and suddenly, he couldn't breathe, couldn't think, couldn't wait.

He slipped his fingers beneath the edges of the thong, feathering through the tight little curls to the soft, moist flesh beneath. She was slick and hot, and as her readiness registered, he drew back just far enough to unzip his pants and push them out of the way in a few deft moves, sighing in relief as his throbbing flesh pressed into the satiny bare skin before him.

He reached down and moved himself into position, nudging her legs wider, and she automatically leaned forward, bracing her arms on the small table before which she still stood. Slowly, deliberately, he pressed forward, groaning in relief, delight, ecstasy, as her tight channel admitted him. Forward and forward again, until there was no telling where he left off and she began, until he was snugly embedded within her.

She wriggled a little, searching for a comfortable fit, and he was reminded of how new she was to this. Tenderness swept him, and he slid his palm around to her abdomen, flattening it there and extending a seeking finger down over the soft rise of her mons until he found the pouting bud between her legs.

She cried out when he gently pressed it, and he smiled as he initiated a circling pattern of magic that quickly had her moving and shifting in his arms.

He paused for a moment, and she said, "Adam!" in a threatening tone. And then she rolled her hips once, twice, and he was lost. Beginning a slow steady rhythm, he clung grimly to control, but she wouldn't let him wait, and as her body writhed and shifted on him, he felt the control slipping away, vanishing in the mist of passion, and he began to move faster and faster, bare flesh slapping against bare flesh. He anchored her to him with his hand on her abdomen, and their movements pressed his finger hard against her, making her cry out again and again until, with a near-scream of incoherent pleasure, she began to convulse in his arms. Her body shook and surged, tightened around him in a sensual grip he was powerless to resist. Faster and higher the tight coil of tension within him flew until he felt shivers of completion rushing along his spine, surging down to empty him into her in final great thrusts that arched his back and left him spent and gasping, curved over her back as she lay across the table.

For long moments, neither of them spoke. Finally, he stepped back, reluctantly disengaging their bodies. Selene still didn't move, and he took a second to fasten his pants before moving to her side and drawing her to him. She circled his arms with her neck, then squeaked in surprise as he bent and scooped her into his arms.

He bent his head and kissed her, lingering over the sweetness of the moment. "Sorry," he said when he lifted his head. "I think we got a few things out of order."

She smiled up at him, laying her head against his shoulder as he began to carry her up the stairs. "And we forgot something, too."

Adam stopped dead, shock ripping through him. What the hell had he been thinking? He'd completely forgotten about birth control! "Oh, hell," he said. "I never gave it a thought."

"It's all right." She stroked his face with her fingers, appearing amazingly calm and unaffected under the circumstances.

"How is it all right?" he demanded. "If you get pregnant—"

"We'll deal with it together," she said, still nonchalant. "It would make all this worrying about keeping it from my father until after the election seem a lot less of a problem, wouldn't it?" There was actually a note of humor in her voice.

"It isn't funny!" he said.

"It is," she said, openly laughing now. "*You're* funny. I've never seen you so panicked."

"With good reason." But he was relaxing again as he started on up the stairs, and a smile tugged at his lips.

He set her on her feet in his bathroom, keeping one arm around her as he reached in to turn on the shower. Then he turned to her, tugging the sweater over her head and tossing it onto the wide counter.

Her eyes widened as he unhooked her bra. "We're going to shower together?"

He grinned. "Yeah." And with that, he stripped off the rest of their clothes and tugged her into the shower. "And this time we're using protection. Much as I like the idea of you having my baby, the timing would really be lousy."

She softened, curling into his arms and pulling his head down for a kiss. "Make love to me again. With or without protection."

Afterward, they toweled each other dry and he led her into his bedroom. "I've wanted you here," he confessed, "in my bed."

"I can't stay," she said. But she let him pull back the sheets and lay her down.

He gathered her into his arms and tugged the sheets over them, creating a cozy cocoon. "Just for a few minutes." He stroked her back. "I love you, Selene."

She stilled in his arms. For a long moment she didn't speak, and resignation seeped through him. She was determined not to let him tie any strings between them until after this damned election.

Then she said, "I love you, too." She tilted her head back and kissed his chin. "If I'm pregnant—which I doubt—I promise I'll tell you right away."

"And we'll get married right away."

She smiled. "You know, I should be worried. You're just sneaky enough to get me pregnant and force the issue."

He grinned. "Much as I'd like to plan something like that, I'll only insist if it turns out we have a baby on the way. If not, we'll wait until after the election."

She hesitated, her pretty face growing serious. "I'm sorry I've been so difficult about our relationship. I don't want you to be unhappy."

"It's okay," he murmured. And it was. She loved him. She loved him enough to actually hold a discussion about marriage and children. About their future together. Knowing that, he could wait seven weeks to share her with the world.

Two hours later the telephone trilled, jarring him out of a daze. As he reluctantly released Selene and reached for the handset, he glanced at the clock. Twelve-thirty. Who in hell would be calling him after midnight? Dread coalesced in his belly, the dread that inevitably accompanied such a late call. Something must have happened to someone in his family.

He sat up in the bed. "Hello?"

"Adam. Thank God you're home." It was his father.

"What's wrong?" he demanded.

"It's Marcus," his father said in a voice filled with more fear and concern than Adam had ever heard him use before. "He's been arrested."

"Arrested?"

"Yes. For racketeering."

"Rack—? That's ridiculous and they know it. I thought this was settled the last time they questioned him."

"Apparently we were wrong." His father's voice was worried. "Ian is sure it's a frame-up."

"The cartel." He knew immediately. "They haven't been able to pressure Ian into switching to their coffee bean exporters any other way." He was already scrambling out of bed. "Call a lawyer. I'm on my way."

"Marc already has. He called some friend from the bar association who will do for the bail hearing, but he's going to need more than that. Ian's calling Jake and the rest of the family. I'll meet you at the police station. I'm going to push to get him released tonight. We can straighten the charges out tomorrow."

"All right. I'll be there."

Adam and his father disconnected simultaneously. He tossed the phone in the general direction of the bedside table as he grabbed fresh suit pants from his closet.

"What's wrong?" Selene was sitting in the middle of the bed, apprehension etched on her pretty face.

"My brother's been arrested. Marc—the one you met. They're saying he's involved in racketeering. I've got to get down to the police station." He thrust his arms into the sleeves of a dress shirt and frantically buttoned it, before stuffing the shirttails into his pants.

Selene jumped out of bed and tossed on his robe, hanging on the back of the bathroom door. "Is there anything I can do?"

"No." His mind was caroming in a dozen different directions as he belted the pants and knotted a tie around his neck, then slipped into his suit jacket. "Yes. Get yourself home. Take your time, just lock the door on your way out." He picked up his wallet, keys and cell phone and grabbed the briefcase that contained his laptop. He strode to the door where she waited, pausing briefly.

She wore his robe but she hadn't tied it, and as frantic as he was, he couldn't resist sliding one hand inside and pulling her to him, fondling the smooth, bare curves as he lingered over a final kiss. "I love you. I'll call when I can."

"I love you, too." She stepped back and nodded her head at the door. "Go. Hurry."

That night, back in her own bed after leaving Adam's silent, lonely home, she didn't sleep well at all. His words kept ringing in her ears. *My brother's been arrested.*

Of course it must have been a mistake. Adam hadn't believed it for a minute, she reminded herself.

But if she'd heard Adam correctly, it wasn't a mistake, but a deliberate act by persons in a cartel. Which implied drugs.

At six-thirty she rose and dressed, then went down to the breakfast room. Normally she didn't eat this early but she knew the morning papers arrived before seven and she was anxious to see if anything about Marcus Danforth had gotten into the early editions. Although she'd spoken encouragingly to Adam last night, she had known from the grim expression on his face that his brother's arrest was cause for real concern.

As she entered the room, her father was just taking his seat at the table. "Good morning, Father," she said.

"Good morning, Selene. You're up early."

It wasn't a question so she didn't volunteer a response, merely smiled and nodded as she made a bee-line for the table. The papers lay in a neatly stacked pile beside her father's place, and she glanced at them long-ingly. She couldn't pounce on them and scan the front page without making him suspicious.

Slowly, she took a seat across from him. The house-keeper bustled in with coffee.

"So." Her father shook open his newspaper without looking at it as he glanced measuringly over the top of it at her. "You were out late last night."

"You must have gotten home earlier than usual," she countered, "because I wasn't really late at all. I'm usually in bed by the time you stagger in."

Her father's eyebrows rose. "It was after midnight."

"In Europe, parties are just getting started at mid-night. I tend to forget how provincial the States can be." She smiled. "It will be wonderful to be in France again when my friend Willi gets married."

"Just for a visit, right?" Her father lowered his paper an inch.

She shrugged, reaching for the silver coffee carafe. "Who knows?" Her father, above all else, craved control. This inquisition into her personal life wasn't really *personal,* she reminded herself. He wasn't really interested in her; it was simply an exercise in ownership. And she knew the only way to make him back down was the im-plied threat that if he continued to probe, she would leave.

"Well," he finally said, rustling his papers. "I had hoped after the election that we could spend more time together."

She sent him a bland smile and stirred her coffee. "As had I."

Stalemate.

As her father finally turned his attention to the paper, Selene held out a hand as if she weren't particularly interested. "Would you hand me one of those, please?"

"What section?"

"I don't care. Front page, I suppose. I really should keep up with the campaign developments."

Her father reached absently for another newspaper, but as his gaze fell on the above-the-fold headline, she saw him freeze in midmotion.

"Whoo-*hoo!*"

She jumped a foot in the air, her hand going automatically to her throat as her father continued to hoot and cackle. "What on earth is the matter?" she asked, raising her voice to be heard over his jubilant celebration. She watched him warily, half expecting him to leap to his feet for a victory dance.

He turned the paper so she could see the headline. "One of those damned Danforths has been arrested!"

She snatched the paper from his hand and rapidly skimmed the article. Over her father's noise, she saw that the article told her little more than Adam had the night before. Marcus Danforth, fourth son of prominent politician and senatorial candidate Abraham Danforth, had been arrested, charged with racketeering by the FBI.

"This will sink Danforth's campaign," her father sneered. "He's managed to wriggle out of the last couple of sticky spots the press has caught him in, but there's no way to whitewash this."

"Unless it's a mistake," she said quietly. "He hasn't been found guilty yet."

"It won't matter," her father predicted. "There are fewer than two months left now until the election. Danforth's not going to be able to bounce back that fast." He rubbed his hands together. "This couldn't have come at a better time."

"I'm sure Marcus Danforth doesn't share your sentiments." She shook her head sadly. "I don't care how it affects the campaign. I refuse to wish ill luck on anyone just for the sake of winning."

"That's not what I meant," her father said impatiently.

"Oh?" She reached for a slice of toast and began to spread butter over the top. "Then what did you mean? It sounded like you were pleased that this poor man has been arrested because the resulting bad publicity would further your political goals."

"Well, perhaps, but—"

"What are you going to do if you don't win?" she asked.

Her father stopped talking. Stopped smiling. "What?"

She repeated the question.

"What kind of a thing is that to ask me?" he demanded. "Don't you have any faith in your own father?"

She ignored the aggressive tone. "Of course I do, but there can only be one winner. I honestly want to know what you plan to do if you aren't the one the voters elect."

John Van Gelder looked at his daughter with a blank expression. "It's never occurred to me that I wouldn't win," he said simply.

She realized he was telling her the exact truth—he had never even considered losing.

"But what if you do?" she persisted.

He frowned at her again. "I don't know. I suppose I'd…get involved in a business again." But he didn't sound certain.

Pain pierced her heart. *Don't be silly,* she lectured herself. *Surely you weren't expecting him to say something about spending more time with you?* "Well," she said crisply, "maybe you'd better think about it a little bit. In the unlikely event that you lose—" she worked hard to keep any hint of sarcasm out of her voice "—you might want to have some future plan to share with the press. Otherwise, you're liable to look ridiculously foolish, or conceited, or both."

She turned her attention back to the paper she held, aware that her father was gaping at her. No wonder. She'd never spoken to him like that before in their entire, albeit limited, history.

At the bottom of the article about Adam's brother was a small, italicized sentence: *See related story, p. 4C.*

Page 4C? That was the society section. The gossip corner. As always, during a hotly contested election, the media scavenged for any juicy tidbits they could find. As she flipped to the fourth page of the section, she idly wondered what they'd found now. Given the number of people in Adam's extended family, it was a sure bet there were plenty of skeletons hidden in closets. And probably a number of perfectly innocent mistakes that could be made to look far worse than they ever had been, as well.

But as she caught sight of the article, her brain stopped functioning and shut down altogether.

It was a photo of Adam and her. Together. Coming out of the hotel where they'd spent their first glorious night.

So shocked she couldn't even react, she simply sat and stared at the damaging photo.

They had just come through the front door of the small hotel; its sign was clearly visible just to their left. Adam had one arm around her. In the other, he carried her small overnight case. He was smiling down into her upturned face, an unmistakably tender expression that she might have been pleased to see under different circumstances. A large caption with bold type below the photo read: *Danforth-Van Gelder Campaign Takes Intimate Turn.*

There was an accompanying article. She scanned it automatically, a sick, lurching feeling growing inside her.

Abe Danforth's youngest son might be under siege, but his third son has reportedly made friends with the enemy. Adam Danforth was seen escorting heiress Selene Van Gelder, daughter of his father's chief rival for the senate seat, from a well-known historic hotel recently. This Danforth son, while still a bachelor, has been seen in the company of heiresses before, most notably with the former Karis Dougherty...

The rest of the article was even more scurrilous. There was a picture of Adam—clearly a much younger Adam—carrying a woman in his arms, standing on the stoop of what looked to be a private home. The article explained that Karis Dougherty had been engaged at the time the picture had been taken, that Adam insisted that it had been nothing more than a study date for which he'd offered to give her a ride. It ended with arch insinuations that made her heart ache for Adam and infuriated her. No wonder he'd been so determined that they share the news with the press at their own pace. This made something so special seem…cheap and ugly.

She had barely absorbed the article when her father said, "What in hell is this?" It was a roar of anger and she knew he'd found either the same or a similar article in the edition he was reading. "Selene, there'd better be a damn good reason for you to be in a photo looking intimate with Adam Danforth. This could ruin the campaign!"

She tore her gaze away from the paper. "How could it possibly hurt your campaign?" she asked wearily. She'd feared that if her father found out about her relationship with Adam, he'd go ballistic. It was disheartening to be right.

"Are you telling me you're…seeing this boy?" Her father stood, papers sliding sideways to the floor. His face was red with rage. "He's a *Danforth!*"

"I know that, Father. I have yet to discover what's so objectionable about the family, other than the fact that you're running against one of them for office." Her own voice was louder.

"Abe Danforth," John gritted, "is a philandering wastrel. He had designs on your mother's fortune years ago, until her family got wise to him."

There was a stunned silence in the room. She could see in her father's eyes that he hadn't intended to blurt that out. And of all the things she'd expected him to say, that hadn't even been among the possibilities. "He…what?"

"He was one of your mother's suitors many years ago," her father said stiffly.

"Before you?"

He nodded once.

"Did you know her then?"

He nodded again, his eyes softening. "She was the most beautiful of the debutantes that year. I loved her the moment I saw her." His gaze was distant. "Every man in the room did. But none of them could get near her after Abe Danforth set eyes on her."

Suddenly, the reasons for her father's antipathy toward Abraham Danforth made sense. Not good sense, given that the events must have occurred nearly forty years ago, but at least she understood the connection at last. "But she married you," she prompted.

"Yes, after her father put a stop to an unsuitable alliance with the Danforths."

"Why was it unsuitable? The Danforth fortune puts ours in the shade, so he can't really have been after her money. I don't understand. Were they related?"

John Van Gelder shook his graying head. "No, nothing like that. Abe's father had gotten the better of your grandfather in business on a number of occasions. There was bad blood between them."

Bad blood between them. And her father appeared to have carried on the grudge.

So her mother had been forbidden to see Abraham Danforth. Her father's antipathy became even clearer— he hadn't been her first choice and he knew it. Had she loved Abe? Had she simply accepted the first man who came along after the relationship was forcibly ended? Selene doubted she would ever know, but she felt a surprising pang of pity for her father. He'd clearly adored her mother…and probably had never known if she cared for him in the same way.

"We intended to talk to you after the election was over," she said. "I didn't want to upset you while you had so much going on with the campaign."

"We?" Her father's face darkened again. "Selene, I forbid you to see Adam Danforth again."

She stared at him. Was he serious? Didn't he understand that words like those were what tore families apart? "You'd better be careful about what you say," she warned him. "I never would have met Adam if it weren't for you—"

"Me? How?"

"That stupid fund-raiser at Twin Oaks," she reminded him. "You insisted I attend. I met Adam there, remember?" She lowered her head and glared at her father. "And I have no intention of allowing you to dictate whom I see." She glanced back at the paper. "I can't imagine how they got this photo. Surely there aren't media hounds following all the members of the Danforth family around. There must be dozens of them!"

It was only chance that led her to glance back at her father.

He had an odd expression on his face. Almost a guilty one, if she wasn't mistaken. A little alarm bell began ringing hectically in her mind. "You didn't," she said slowly, "have anything to do with this, did you?"

"Er, no." Her father wasn't a good liar.

"You did!" She rose, facing him across the table. "Tell me you didn't set me up for this photo op."

"Of course not!" This time, truth rang in his tone. Then, as she watched, he seemed to deflate like a slowly leaking balloon. "Not on purpose, anyway." He sighed. "I hired a private investigator to follow you and report back to me. I was concerned when you began spending so much time away from home."

She was beyond appalled. "You hired someone to take pictures of me and Adam just because you have an imaginary grudge against Abraham Danforth? Are you *crazy?*" She never shouted. But she was shouting now.

Her father seemed to shrink in upon himself even further. "I didn't know who you were seeing when I hired him."

With each new revelation her shock and fury swelled. "That shouldn't have mattered! You hired someone to snoop on your own daughter instead of simply asking me who I was going out with?" She laughed wildly, bitterly. "You got more than you bargained for, didn't you?" She regarded him as if he were a very small and very repellent bug on her breakfast plate. "I will never forgive you for this." She spoke very slowly and very distinctly, each word quivering with the rage she couldn't repress. "I have spent most of my life wondering what was wrong with me to make you dislike me so. I got used to being ignored. I suffered through this damned campaign because you needed a family prop to make you look good. I even went to your opponent's fund-raiser because you insisted—and guess what? I met Adam Danforth there. I fell in love with someone you hate just because of his last name."

"Selene, I—"

"And here's another newsflash for you, Father. I do not intend to stop seeing Adam. Ever. He wants to marry me." She shook her head. "My own father spying on me."

"I asked him specifically not to take pictures," John said quietly. "The man must have recognized your— Adam—and decided he could make more money with those than he could working for me." Then her words sank in and his eyes widened. "You're going to *marry* him?"

"I am." She started for the door of the breakfast room, then turned and regarded her father again. "And do not assume you'll be invited to the wedding." She stomped out, slamming the door behind her. She'd never lost her temper like that in her life, as far as she could remember. Her hands were shaking and her insides were quivering. She felt like she was going to cry. Or throw up. Or both.

And dear heaven, she needed to call Adam right away. What on earth would he think when he saw that? She knew how he felt about publicity. The jelly in her stomach congealed into a hard ball as she ran to find her phone.

Nine

Adam had been asleep less than two hours when someone knocked on his door. He rolled over and peered at the alarm clock, but when he saw the clunky old clock of his boyhood rather than the more modern one that graced his bedside table at his own home, memory flooded back.

He was at Crofthaven, in his boyhood room. His father hadn't really done much with the house in the more than fifteen years since Adam had left home. While the more public areas that visitors saw were periodically refurbished, the bedrooms that belonged to the kids hadn't been changed much.

A second rap sounded on the door. More forceful. Impatient, maybe.

"Come in," he called. He sat up, scrubbing his hands over his face. When he saw the familiar features of his younger brother Marcus, relief joined the parade of memories from the night before. It had been several hours until they'd been allowed to take Marcus home from the police station. Anxious hours during which the lawyer Marc had retained had refused to let Marcus or any of them speak to the FBI, hours during which they hadn't been permitted to so much as see him. It had taken all the Danforth influence as well as a ridiculously sizable bail to get him out. "How are you?" he asked.

Marc's handsome face was sober. But he'd clearly showered and looked a lot better than he'd looked hours earlier when Adam had brought him home. He tossed the morning paper onto the edge of Adam's bed. "How would you be if you were arrested for something you didn't do?" he asked.

Adam grimaced. "Point taken." He eyed his brother. "Family support is one thing, bro, but you'd better be in here for a damned good reason. I didn't get to sleep until after five. And it's barely seven now. What's up? Have you heard something?"

Marc shook his head. "No." He hesitated. "There's something in the paper you need to see."

His brother's manner stirred Adam's nerve endings to alert. "Such as?" He pushed himself up straighter.

Marcus silently reached for the paper and handed it to him. Adam noted that the front page had been folded back to a section inside. His brother pointed to an article and photos near the top of the page.

At the first glimpse of the photo, Adam couldn't believe what he was seeing. He remembered the morning

well, the feel of Selene's slim shoulder as he hugged her
against his side, the way she'd laughed up into his face.
He even remembered consciously restraining himself
from leaning down and kissing her because they were
in public…and the whole time, someone had been
skulking in the shadows with a camera.

Selene's father was going to flip out. He forced himself to read the article, his features hardening in disgust.
Of course they had to drag that old story up. Poor Karis.
Her husband George was going to be livid, too. When
the story had broken a decade ago, he'd nearly called
off the engagement. But Adam and Karis had finally
been able to explain the misunderstanding, and Karis's
wedding had gone forward as planned. The couple still
lived in the Savannah area and George wasn't going to
be happy at this latest smearing of his wife's character.

Character smearing. His father's campaign was
going to take a hit from this mess with Marcus, and to
have Adam falsely broadcast across the media as a play-
boy wasn't going to help. John Van Gelder must be dancing a jig this morning if he'd seen this article, even if
he was furious that Selene was involved with Adam.

If he was furious…how far would Selene go to earn
her only parent's love? Although he despised himself for
it, he couldn't banish the stirrings of suspicion that
curled around the edges of his mind.

Adam thought of the pain in her eyes, the longing that
lingered in her tone when she spoke of her father despite
the flashes of resentment he'd also seen. It was obvious
she'd never felt loved. What, he wondered, would she
do to gain his attention, his approval?

And then the cold, unwanted thought he'd been fruitlessly trying to evade exploded in his brain. Could she possibly have planned all this?

He remembered his shock when he'd learned her last name. He'd been too caught up in the romance of the moment to ask what a Van Gelder had been doing at his father's campaign event, but he'd wondered about it off and on ever since. He'd intended to ask Selene but he'd forgotten. Several times.

His mouth tightened into a grim line as he recalled why he'd forgotten, the explosive passion they'd shared, their last happy discussion of a future complete with children. Had it all been an act?

Another knock on the half-open door interrupted his anguished thoughts, and he and Marcus both turned as their father strode in. He carried another copy of the paper, folded back to the same page at which Adam had been staring.

"Are you all right?" Abe's voice was gentle.

Adam swallowed. He shook his head. "I don't know. God, Dad, I'm sorry. This can't be good for the campaign."

Abe shrugged. "There are things in life a lot more important than the campaign." He held up the paper. "I didn't even know you knew her."

There was a long moment of silence in the room.

Finally, Adam admitted the hard truth. "Apparently, I didn't."

Marc stirred. "How, exactly, did you two meet?"

Adam swallowed. "She was at the Twin Oaks fundraiser in July."

Both his father's and his brother's eyes went wide with disbelief.

"What was she doing there?" Marc demanded.

"I don't know. I didn't think to ask her at the time, and since then, I keep forgetting when I'm with her." It sounded unbelievably naive and feeble when he said it aloud. "I'm sorry, Dad."

There was a silence in the room.

Then his father chuckled. "Women have a way of making you forget any common sense you have. I knew Selene's mother. If the daughter is half as beautiful, no wonder you forgot."

"Oh, she's beautiful," Marc growled. "On the outside, at least."

Adam felt too sick to speak.

Abe laid a hand on Adam's shoulder and squeezed briefly. "Don't worry about it. If people are so easily swayed by ridiculous tabloid stories that they choose not to vote for me, then so be it."

He swallowed. "But I don't want to cost you votes," he said, "and I may have been stupid enough to—"

"Adam," said his father, "is—was she important to you?"

Was oxygen important to breathing?

Before he could answer, Marc nodded his head. "Yeah," he said quietly. "She was."

His father and brother left the room again, but Adam barely realized they'd left. Numbly, he picked up the offensive newspaper again, looking at Selene's smiling face. Sharp claws of pain ripped at his heart. He'd thought she really cared for him. He'd thought he'd finally found a woman who didn't want anything from him, didn't need anything except his love.

He'd been wrong. Again.

Selene was growing more frantic as the day wore on. Since she'd walked away from the breakfast table that morning she'd been trying to get hold of Adam without success. She'd called his home repeatedly, had left several messages there as well as on his cell phone. There was no answer at his office and the machine merely said that the D&D offices were closed temporarily, that someone would be in the office tomorrow.

Four times, her father had knocked on the locked door of her bedroom suite, but she'd ignored him. If she never saw him again, her life would be perfectly fine. He'd treated her like secondhand goods for her entire life, fobbing her off on others and ignoring her as much as possible. And she'd learned to survive it. But he'd gone too far this time.

How could he have hired someone to report on her movements? The very fact that he didn't appear to understand how bizarre such an action was showed her just how out of touch her father was with the whole concept of being a parent. It had never occurred to him to simply *ask* her where she was going. No, he *paid* someone to report on her. And according to her father, it was simply an unfortunate mistake that the man he'd hired had been unethical and taken photos even though he hadn't been instructed to.

Pain squeezed her heart. If he'd loved her, he never would have let this happen. She shunted aside the pain and concentrated on the hard core of anger settling in her heart. She would never forgive him for this. He'd done something which could harm Adam's family and through them, him.

Adam, she thought on a wave of longing. She couldn't believe he hadn't called her. Was it possible he hadn't seen the picture and accompanying article? She doubted it. More likely, he was holed up somewhere avoiding the media.

God knew, she couldn't blame him if he couldn't contact her right now. Answering the phone had been a nightmare. But she was afraid she might miss a call from Adam if she didn't answer it, and many of the calls couldn't be identified with the caller I.D. screening system. She'd said, "No comment" so many times today that she'd lost track. So she'd suffered through the nosy questions in stony silence each time and simply hung up, hoping that the next time she lifted the handset, she'd hear Adam's voice.

If only she could go to him. But she couldn't leave because there were at least five members of the media camped outside her father's house. And even if she could, where would she go? He wasn't home, he wasn't at his office.

And then it struck her. Crofthaven. He'd gone to his family home. Or possibly to his uncle's. But she'd bet he'd wanted to speak to his father when the news broke, and perhaps he still was there. And she'd completely forgotten his brother's troubles. If Marc was at the family estate, Adam would want to be with him.

New hope flared within her heart. He probably

hadn't called for fear her father would answer. Not because Adam feared her father, but because he would be worried that his call might make things more difficult for her.

Fingers trembling, she found a phone book and looked up the home number for Abraham Danforth.

It rang three times before the connection opened.

An unfamiliar male voice said, "Danforth residence, Whittaker speaking. May I help you?"

"Yes," she said. She had to stop and take a deep breath. "I'd like to speak to Adam, please."

"Who is calling?"

"Selene Van Gelder."

There was a long pause. "Selene Van Gelder?" There was a distinct emphasis on her last name.

"That's correct." Even to her ears, it sounded defiant and she winced. She didn't want anyone in Adam's family to think badly of her.

"Just a moment."

She waited and waited. And waited some more. He must have put her on hold because she heard none of the ordinary noises of a household, no approach of footsteps, nothing. Finally, there was a click and she heard a new voice. "Adam Danforth."

"Adam! I'm so glad I found you. I've left you dozens of messages at your home and on your cell. Are you all right?"

Silence.

Uncertainty assailed her. "Adam?"

"Selene." His voice was oddly flat. "What do you want?"

She was taken aback. "I want to know if you're all right. You had to rush off last night to help Marc and then this morning that odious article—"

"About which you knew nothing, of course." There was a distinct note of sarcasm in his voice now.

"No, I—" She stopped as the tone and the meaning penetrated. "You think I…? Oh, no, Adam, it was my father. He—"

"You, your father, what's the difference?"

Now it was her turn to be silent. He'd never spoken to her like that, faintly accusatory and without a shred of the warmth and intimacy with which his tone usually was imbued. "What," she finally said, very careful to keep her voice neutral, "do you mean, what's the difference between my father and me?"

"Never mind," Adam said. "What were you doing at my father's fund-raiser in July? The one where we so conveniently met?"

He thought she'd set him up. The pain was so sharp and sudden she nearly dropped the telephone. "My father made me go," she said truthfully, knowing it would only nail shut the coffin of his former good opinion of her.

"I see."

No, he didn't see at all. And though a part of her already recognized that it was futile, she loved him so much she had to try to explain. "I didn't want to go," she said, "and I refused to spy on your family, but I said I would attend just to shut him up."

"What a sacrifice," he said. "I suppose you went out with me just to shut him up, too."

"No! You know better than that."

"Do I?"

There was another silence.

"I knew I shouldn't get involved with you," she said. "I knew my father wasn't rational in his dislike of your family. But when I saw your note, I couldn't stop thinking about how perfect that night had been…"

"Perfect, all right. It was the perfect opportunity to do something that would get you into your father's good graces."

"No!" She was growing frantic. "I only wanted to be with you."

"You wanted," he said deliberately, "to do anything that would make your father notice you."

That was when she realized how hopeless it was. His voice was cold and hard, completely unlike the man she'd grown to love.

"What happens now?" She pressed the back of her hand against her mouth to hold back the sobs that made her throat ache.

"Nothing," he said. "Nothing at all." And the receiver on his end went dead.

Selene clung to the receiver, pressing it against her ear. Her last link to Adam. Finally, feeling as if she would break if she wasn't very, very cautious, she pressed the button and killed the buzzing of the disconnect sound that was all he'd left her. Slowly she set the handset down. Then, very carefully, she lay down across her bed and laid her head on her crossed arms as the tears began to flow.

Adam thought she'd betrayed him. On purpose. Funny, but to her the concept of betrayal had always had some sort of medieval overtone. She'd grown up in Europe, where generations had fought over lands since ancient times, and where betrayal of family and fealty featured prominently in many of the old tales. Now, however, it had become very modern and very real.

Her father had betrayed her trust and the unconditional love she'd offered. And in doing so, he'd ruined her chance at a future with the man she loved.

Adam thought she'd betrayed the love and trust he'd offered her. Did he really believe she wanted her father's approval so desperately?

Apparently, he did. How had it all gone so wrong?

She cried for a long time, until her duvet was tear-soaked and her emotions were dulled. Until pain had given way to numbness and blank despair. She sat up finally and reached for a tissue, feeling stiff and far older than her years. Sliding off the bed, she looked at her swollen eyes in the mirror. Bleak shadows of loss met her when she gazed into her own eyes.

What was she going to do? She had no reason to stay in Savannah, and yet she had no reason to go, either. There was no one who would miss her, no one to welcome her.

And then she thought of Willi. Of Paris. An ocean away from the memories that would haunt her forever if she stayed here. Picking up the phone, she dialed the airlines. The earliest flight out was tomorrow just after eleven.

She took it.

He didn't go home that night.

For one thing, there were reporters everywhere, according to Ian and Jake. Marc had decided to brave the hordes and had escaped earlier in the company of his female bodyguard. Emphasis on *body,* Adam thought with perhaps the one real flash of humor he'd felt all day. His brother had seemed more alert and alive in the short hours since he'd met his attractive new body-guard—more as if he gave a damn whether he lived or died—than he had in a year.

The house was stifling him. He wished he could leave like Marc had, but the sad truth was that he really had nowhere to go. If he went home, he'd just be hounded by the press. And he'd already screwed things up enough for the old man without courting more trouble.

Courting…he stepped through the French doors onto the terrace, closing them gently behind him. When he was a child and the house had become too oppressive, he'd escaped in this very same manner. He walked across the perfect lush green of the lawn, prettier now in early autumn than it had been during the heat of the summer, and headed past the gardens, past the peach orchard into the grove of trees at the far edge of the property.

As a child, he'd spent hours beneath the cool, dark canopy of leafy branches festooned with Spanish moss. Even then, he'd been convinced he'd see the ghost that had haunted the property since the time of his great-grandfather Hiram.

Today, for the first time he could remember, he didn't even bother looking around as he stomped his way along the path. The trees gave way to massive bayberry and other shrubs as he neared the cliff above the property's private beach, but he didn't intend to go that far. He liked the solemn anonymity of the forested land.

All he could think of was Selene, which was the height of stupidity after what she'd done. How could he have been so wrong about her? The night they'd met, he'd felt an astonishing sense of rightness with her that he'd never felt with any other woman. Certainly he'd never felt it with Angela—that had been nothing more than a crush. He was even more grateful to have escaped *that* mistake now that he knew what a real, loving relationship should entail.

But you don't, he reminded himself brutally. *You don't have any idea what a real relationship would be like. You've been living a lie with a woman who was using you.*

But his anger had begun to fade, replaced by a sweeping sadness that pervaded his thoughts and sapped his energy. Had it really all been a lie? He'd been so sure of her love.

And she'd sounded so miserable on the phone. If she'd truly intended to string him along for the sake of making him look like a philandering fool in the media, why had she been so upset? For that matter, why had she called him at all? She had to know he'd figure it out, realize that she'd only been with him in an effort to dredge up gossip and tarnish his father's campaign.

He snorted. She'd gone awfully far. What would she have done if the media hadn't picked up this story? Accused him of rape?

The pain he'd buried returned with a vengeance and he sank down onto a fallen tree trunk along the side of the path, putting his head in his hands.

"Adam." It was a mere whisper of sound but it scared the hell out of him. He'd thought he was alone. He leaped to his feet, realizing even as he did so that at the far side of the clearing was something he'd never seen before in his life. Goose bumps rose along his arms, prickled up the back of his neck and along his scalp.

A young woman stood on the far side of the small clearing where he'd stopped to sit. But she was no ordinary young woman. She was barely visible, a mere cloud shimmering in the afternoon light and he swallowed as he realized he could see right through her to the shrubby undergrowth behind her.

She wore a traveling cloak from decades past over a floor-length gown. What little he could see of the dress was modest and unassuming, and she carried a small ladies' bag and a bonnet over one arm. Her hair appeared to be dark and was parted down the middle and tightly pulled back from her face, woven into a braided twist that was anchored at the back of her head. Strangely, despite the fragile appearance of the…the vision, or whatever she was, her pretty features were plainly visible. She was young. Very young, probably not even twenty, he'd guess, if one could apply age to a…a ghost.

His mouth was dry as a dust. His heart was thumping as if it would jump right out of his chest. For all the times he'd longed to see a ghost, it had never occurred to him that such an encounter would scare the pants off him. "Who are you?" he managed.

"Priscilla Carlisle."

He was caught by her eyes, gazing straight at him

with an expression of ineffable sadness. "Miss Carlisle." He realized, even as he said it, who she was. "The governess."

She nodded somberly. "You know of me."

"Only a little. You were hired by Hiram Danforth. But as your coach arrived, a fierce storm hit. Your carriage overturned and you—you died." He nearly pinched himself, just to make sure he wasn't dreaming. He was *talking to a ghost*!

She nodded again, and he had the sense that she was pleased. "There is more."

"More?" He was confused. "But that's all I know." He hesitated. "We know you were buried here."

She turned and looked back over her shoulder. "He planted a tree for me."

"Who planted a tree for you?"

She looked back at him and her eyes were deep wells of sorrow. "My father."

"Your...?" He didn't understand. "Who was your father?" Had she been the child of one of Hiram's servants? He'd had several, although to their knowledge, he'd never owned slaves but had paid for the labor he needed. "Were you from a local family?"

"My father," she said, "was Hiram Danforth."

"Hiram Danforth? But he was my grandfather. He was married."

She very nearly smiled and he sensed her amusement. "Yes," she said, "he was. But not to *my* mother."

"Ah. I see."

"I was coming here to live at his request," she continued. "My mother was a maid in his family home in

Boston when he was a young man. A match between them was out of the question. She was an Irish indentured servant; he was the only son of a wealthy industrialist."

"Did they care for each other?" Adam dared to ask.

"I don't know," she said. "I like to think so. My mother died in an influenza epidemic, but Hiram made sure I was kept with the household. He even saw to it that I received an education. Of course, he eventually married and came south. When his children were of school age, he asked me to come and live with him as a governess. It was a good opportunity," she said, "for an orphan with no protection and no prospects. And it was a chance to be near my father."

Adam considered her story. Very practical, he imagined. In the 1890s there was little tolerance for marriage outside one's social class. Then something occurred to him. "Hiram never told anyone you were his daughter, did he?"

She shook her head and he felt another wave of sadness permeate the air around him. "He couldn't," she said simply.

He was astonished at the wave of emotion he felt. "So all these years," he said, "more than a century, you've just wanted…"

"To be part of the family." She nodded.

"You've tried to speak to so many people. Why me?"

"You're the first one who *wanted* to speak to me," she said, a slight smile lightening her features. "I have waited for you for a very long time."

Somehow, he knew what to do. He stood, made a formal bow that amazingly didn't feel silly at all. "Priscilla

Carlisle," he said, "welcome to the Danforth family. Our home is your home."

The diaphanous figure in front of him literally brightened before his eyes, and he had to squint at the radiance that shone from her. "Thank you, Adam," she said. And as he watched, the ghostly form began to fade from sight, until the small clearing in which he sat looked no more remarkable than any other forested glade on any other afternoon.

The pervasive sadness was gone, and a peaceful quality had taken its place. With a sense of certainty he didn't even question, he knew the ghost of Crofthaven had been seen for the last time.

Ten

That night after dark, Adam returned to his own home. Most of the media frenzy surrounding Marc's arrest and his own splash as a subject of gossip had died down and the few reporters still on the story were easy to ignore.

Harder to ignore were the questions rolling around inside his head. How could she have done that to him? Had she ever really loved him or had it all been an act?

After his unbelievable encounter that afternoon, he'd rushed back along the path the way he'd come. His mind had been racing, eager to get back to the house and write it down. He'd had a moment's wild thought: *Imagine what Selene will say when—*

And then it had come back to him again. He wouldn't be telling Selene.

The extraordinary encounter had erased his troubles

from his mind for a few brief moments. But as the memory of the photo from the paper came rushing back, he tasted bitter disillusionment again.

Something was bothering him, though. Something even more than missing her as if she were a limb he'd had amputated. More than the betrayal that still stung every time he cautiously nudged around the edges of the memory.

I love you, too, she'd told him. She was either one of the best actresses on the planet or she'd meant the words. He couldn't have been mistaken about that. God, she'd been a virgin! Why had she ever let things go so far between them if all he'd been to her was a means to an end?

The only answer was that it meant more than that to her, too. But if that were true, then why in hell had she gone along with her father's scheming?

The only way he would ever know, he decided, was to ask her. He glanced at his watch, noting that it was nearly ten, but it didn't matter now that he'd determined he needed to find out what was going on in her head.

Steeling himself for the encounter, he picked up the phone and called the Van Gelder home. He called the house rather than her cell phone, which he'd often seen her turn off when she wasn't expecting any calls. This was going to be difficult enough without the problematic reception cell phones sometimes encountered, anyway.

"Van Gelder residence." The voice was rough and aggressive and Adam felt his hackles rise. He'd bet his life he was speaking to John Van Gelder himself.

"This is Adam Danforth," he said. "May I please—?"

"Danforth!" The word was explosive. "Where's my daughter?"

Adam was completely dumbfounded. "Isn't she at home? I called to speak with her."

There was a heavy silence on the other end of the telephone. "She's not with you?" the man asked suspiciously.

"I haven't seen her since before my brother was arrested. Since before I read the news," Adam said evenly. "Are you telling me you don't know where she is?"

"That's correct." The words sounded as if they were being pulled from Van Gelder's throat. "We had an argument after she saw the paper this morning and she spent the day in her room. Wouldn't talk to me," he admitted. "I tried again at dinnertime but she was gone. The maid said she took a bag with her and got in a cab but Selene didn't tell anyone here where she was going."

"And you haven't called in your private investigator to track her down?" The moment the words were out he regretted them, but the anger was too close to the surface to be completely controlled.

Surprisingly, Selene's father didn't slam down the phone or take offense as he expected. Instead, the man sighed. "I deserve that. And I can assure you the last thing I would do is call a private investigator to report on my daughter's movements again."

Again. A chill rippled down Adam's spine as the words registered. "What?"

"I said I would never—"

"I heard you. Selene didn't know you'd gotten some-one to take pictures of her?"

"I didn't," John said testily. "In fact, I specifically told him no pictures. I just wanted to know where she was going. I guess the S.O.B. thought he'd make a quick buck on the side when he realized who she was with."

"Selene didn't know about the P.I.?"

"No. Wha—oh, hell." Her father sounded truly dis-tressed. "Did you think—?"

"Yeah." Adam leaned his forehead against the wall and closed his eyes. God. She'd tried to tell him, but he wouldn't listen. A sick feeling blossomed in his stom-ach and spread through his system as he realized what he'd done.

"Look," he said to her father. "Can you think of any friends, anyone she might have called? The only friend she's ever spoken of to me is Guillemette, her school roommate who lives in Paris."

"Yes, Willi. She's the only one I know, as well," John said. "Do you think…?"

"I'll check the flights to Paris. If she didn't leave the house until late afternoon, she probably didn't catch a flight out today. She may be spending the night in a hotel, planning to leave in the morning." Adam paused. "Can you call Guillemette?"

"All right, but what do you have in mind?"

Adam took a deep breath. He decided he might as well ask for the moon. The worst the man could do was refuse to help. "Mr. Van Gelder, I love your daughter. I want to marry her. I don't know exactly what your re-lationship has been in the past but I know Selene wants—needs—you in her life."

"And I want her in mine!" Van Gelder sounded desperate. "Selene means a lot to me. More than I've let myself realize until recently. I lost her mother when she was a baby and it…kept me from letting Selene become too important, I guess. I've spent most of her life shuffling her off to one side, and it was wrong of me. I barely know my own child." He cleared his throat. "I want another chance, if she'll give me one."

"As do I," Adam said quietly.

There was a short silence. Then Van Gelder said, "Maybe a Danforth wouldn't have been my first choice for my daughter, but she says she loves you. If she'll marry you, you have my blessing."

"Good." Adam wished he felt more confident. He was afraid he'd hurt her too badly to deserve forgiveness. He thought again of Priscilla Carlisle—his ancestor, he realized suddenly. She had spent many lonely decades seeking the one thing she'd desired above all else. He would be a complete idiot if he spent the rest of his life—or more—alone and unhappy because he'd been afraid to try to fix the damage he'd done, to try to reclaim the happy life he so wanted with Selene. "What would you do to get her to come back?" he asked.

To his credit, John didn't hesitate. "Anything. I'll even drop out of the senate race if that's what it takes."

"I don't think it will come to that." Adam smiled despite himself. "Here's what I think we should do," he said to the father of the woman he loved.

"Ms. Van Gelder?"

Selene looked up from the magazine that she'd been

staring at for the past half an hour. She sat in a lounge at the Savannah airport, waiting for a flight which would take her first to La Guardia in New York, and then across the Atlantic to Paris. She'd come to the airport hours earlier than she needed to, simply because she'd had no other plans and her mind was too numb to make decisions. She'd barely had enough energy to pack her things and check out of the local hotel into which she'd moved late yesterday when she'd been unable to stand being beneath the same roof as John Van Gelder for one more minute.

Now, right in front of her, an airport employee stood. "Ms. Van Gelder?" the woman said again.

"Yes, I'm Selene Van Gelder." She set aside the magazine and looked up, sighing mentally. Security these days, extremely tight for very good reasons, could still be an amazing pain. What was wrong now?

"Ms. Van Gelder, would you come with me to the VIP lounge, please?"

Selene gathered her purse and carry-on bag. "What's this about?"

"We've been asked to show you something," the woman replied. She turned and began to move away, clearly expecting Selene to follow.

As she walked after the woman, her brow wrinkled at the odd statement. What could they possibly want to show her? Wasn't it usually the other way around?

She followed the airport employee around a corner and down a long corridor into an empty lounge. The woman indicated the comfortable seats scattered around and the coffeemaker along one wall. "Please sit down and make yourself comfortable." Then she pointed to the television on the wall. "This will be coming on in just a moment." And she left Selene alone.

Thoroughly puzzled now, Selene dutifully sat, fidgeting with the strap of her handbag. Then she sat up straighter as the television crackled to life.

The channel flipped to a local morning talk show that she'd often watched. The smiling coanchor was speaking to the television audience as the sound came up.

"...don't know who said the path of true love never runs smoothly, but today we have living proof of that old adage. With me this morning are two gentlemen whom the Savannah audience has probably never expected to see in the same room, much less on the same side of an issue. But this morning, they are united in a common cause. Help me welcome senatorial candidate John Van Gelder and Adam Danforth, the son of Abe Danforth, Van Gelder's chief rival in this race."

The audience dutifully applauded as two men very familiar to her eyes entered the studio and took the guests' seats. They were smiling at the host and looked amazingly comfortable together.

Selene didn't move. She couldn't. Her gaze was riveted to the television. What was going on?

"So," the woman conducting the interview began. "Why don't you tell us, John, what brings you here today."

Her father smiled. He was older and heavier than

he'd been when she was small, but he still had some of that same charisma, and he used it to good effect. "Well, Adam did, literally," he said wryly. After an appreciative laugh from the audience, he went on. "Adam and my daughter Selene have been dating. I only learned about it recently." He sighed. "I'm sure Selene thought I wouldn't be rational about her getting close to any of the Danforth clan and—" his eyebrows rose in self-mockery "—I'm sad to say her instincts probably were right."

"So you didn't want her seeing Adam?" the host inquired.

"I didn't even know she was," John repeated. "But I was concerned because she suddenly began spending a lot of time away from home."

"So what did you do?" The interviewer was relentless.

For the first time, her father looked uncomfortable. "I hired a private investigator to let me know where she was going."

"You *hired* a private investigator?" The woman professed shock. "Isn't that a bit strange? Most fathers would have just asked their daughters, wouldn't they?"

"I'm not most fathers." It was a confession. He almost squirmed in his seat. "Selene's mother passed away when Selene was an infant and I—I had a hard time getting past my grief enough to deal with a child. Selene spent most of her youth at European boarding schools." He shook his head but it didn't look like a rehearsed move. "That was a poor choice, and I've come to regret it."

"Mr. Van Gelder," the interviewer said. "What do

you hope to gain by coming here today with Adam Danforth?"

John spread his hands helplessly. "I want another chance. I'd like Selene to know how sorry I am for the mistakes I've made, and to assure her that I'd like to get to know her."

"How do you know Selene is even listening to this?" the woman asked.

"We don't," said Adam. "We think we may have alerted her to watch, but we're not sure." His broad shoulders seemed to sag a little.

"Short of hiring another investigator," added John, "we have no way of knowing where she is unless she chooses to contact us. And neither one of us is willing to do that, right?" He looked at Adam, and she was stunned anew to see the unspoken moment of understanding that passed between them.

"It has to be her choice," added Adam.

"Is there anything you can say that might induce her to get in touch with you?" The studio host was working every dramatic moment, but Adam and her father didn't seem to notice.

Her father looked down at his hands. Adam nodded.

"Selene, I love you. We both do." He took a deep breath. "Your father and I have made unforgivable mistakes but we're asking you to forgive us, anyway."

Beside him, John fumbled in his pocket. Finally he withdrew something small and handed it to Adam.

It was a small box, she saw as Adam held it up. "This," he said, flipping open the lid, "was Selene's mother's wedding ring. John graciously offered it to me when I asked him for Selene's hand. Selene, will you marry me?"

In the lounge, she gasped as the tears streamed down her face. *Her mother's wedding ring!* How difficult, she wondered, had it been for her father to make that gesture?

In the television studio, Adam smiled straight into the camera. "Meet me in our garden, Selene, and let me put this ring on your finger." His smile wavered just a fraction and his anxiety showed in his eyes. She figured with that tiny lapse, he'd just won the heart of every woman watching. He'd certainly taken hers by storm. "Please?"

The camera narrowed in to focus tightly on his face, then pulled back to reveal John's worried expression. "Well," said the coanchor, "that was certainly one of the more unique proposals I've ever seen. Thank you, gentlemen, for sharing this moment with us and be sure to let us know the lady's response."

As a commercial replaced the faces of the men she loved, Selene leaped to her feet and headed for the door.

Adam paced in the lovely garden behind Twin Oaks. He thought of the night they'd met. It had been dark and mysterious, Selene's eyes sparkling in the shadows. She'd been so beautiful and ethereal in her white gown that even after he'd been assured she was real he still was afraid she was going to vanish.

Had she indeed vanished from his life now, through his own mistrust and stupidity? He wasn't sure what he was going to do if she left for Paris—

And then she was there. Coming down the flagstone

steps from the terrace in a flowing floral-print dress that made her look as exotic as the gardens around them. She stopped in front of him, a few feet away, enormous emerald eyes fixed on his face.

She wasn't smiling. His heart sank, and he steeled himself for the blow of rejection.

There were reporters up on the terrace with cameras. He'd negotiated for space to speak privately in exchange for a full view of the meeting, if it occurred. Either way, they'd have a great story.

For a moment, he was tongue-tied, not knowing what to say. And then the simple truth emerged. "I'm sorry. I wronged you when I failed to trust you."

She nodded. "That hurt."

To his horror, he felt his eyes filling with tears as the pain he'd caused fully registered. "I think, deep down, I believed that I wasn't really interesting enough to hold you, that maybe there did have to be some other reason why you were with me."

She started to speak, but he held up a hand.

"Better let me finish before I can't." His voice was shaking now but he didn't care. "I love you. Can you find it in your heart to forgive me?"

"Of course I forgive you, Adam." But her voice, her expression, was still serious and reserved.

For the first time it occurred to him that her forgiveness and her love might not come hand in hand, and his heart felt like a lead weight in his chest.

"Thank you," she said, "for whatever you said to my father to bring him to his senses."

He shook his head, forcing himself to concentrate on her words. "I didn't. He loves you. He just didn't know how to show it, and honestly, I think he was afraid of caring too much for you. Losing your mother almost destroyed him. He couldn't take a chance on going through that again."

"But life is full of chances," she said.

"He knows that now," he told her, "and he's anxious to start fresh with you."

Silence fell.

"The press is on the terrace," he said. "I had to promise them that in exchange for the television time."

Her eyebrows rose. "What would you have done if I hadn't come?"

He shrugged. "They could have run some great footage of me looking like a total fool."

She smiled faintly. "Lucky for you I showed."

He searched her face. "Is it? You haven't answered me yet."

"What was the question?"

Understanding dawned, and with it the first glimmer of light returned to his world. He reached into his pocket and withdrew a small box. "Since you apparently saw the interview, you know what's in here." He dropped to one knee. "Selene Van Gelder, may I have your hand in marriage?"

She stood stock-still, closed her eyes for a moment, and when she opened them again, she was the one with tears in her eyes. "Yes," she whispered. "Oh, Adam, yes!"

Relief, heady and sweet, poured through him. He stood

and opened his arms, and she came into them without hesitation. Her body was warm and soft and familiar and he pressed her close, seeking her mouth. "I thought I'd ruined things forever," he confessed when he lifted his mouth.

A shout from the terrace distracted them. "Put the ring on her finger, Danforth!"

Adam grinned, turning his head to acknowledge the intrusion. Then he looked down at her, nestled securely in his arms where she belonged. "Shall I?"

"I'd like to wear your ring," she said.

He stepped back a pace and opened the little box. "You did see the whole interview, right? So you know where I got this?"

She smiled tremulously. "Yes. To say I was stunned would be a gross understatement."

"Your father loves you," Adam said. "He knows he needs to work on how to show it." He removed the lovely diamond with its smaller matching stones on each side, and gently worked it onto her ring finger. "This is a symbol of our love, but it's also a symbol of family. Yours, mine and the one I hope we create together."

"Soon," she added, as they admired the ring together.

"As soon as you like." He drew her to him again. "Let's get out of here," he murmured against her mouth. "I don't want an audience for what I want to do with you next."

Selene laughed. "Why do I think I'm going to like it?" She feathered her fingers over the back of his neck and smiled as her hips brushed his.

He shivered as need rushed through him, and drew

away to take her hand. "You'll never believe what happened to me yesterday," he said as he led her out of the garden toward the rest of their lives together.

* * * * *

Don't miss the next book in
DYNASTIES: THE DANFORTHS.
Pick up Linda Conrad's
THE LAWS OF PASSION,
in October.

DYNASTIES: THE DANFORTHS

A family of prominence...
tested by scandal, sustained by passion.

THE LAWS OF PASSION

(Silhouette Desire #1609, available October '04)

by Linda Conrad

When attorney Marcus Danforth was falsely arrested,
FBI agent Dana Aldrich rushed to prove his innocence.
Brought together by the laws of the court, their
intense mutual attraction ignited the laws of passion.
Yet Dana wanted more from this sizzling
hot lawyer—she wanted love....

eHARLEQUIN.com

The Ultimate Destination for Women's Fiction

For **FREE online reading,** visit
www.eHarlequin.com now and enjoy:

Online Reads
Read **Daily** and **Weekly** chapters from
our Internet-exclusive stories by your
favorite authors.

Interactive Novels
Cast your vote to help decide how these
stories unfold...then stay tuned!

Quick Reads
For shorter romantic reads, try our
collection of Poems, Toasts, & More!

Online Read Library
Miss one of our online reads?
Come here to catch up!

Reading Groups
Discuss, share and rave with other
community members!

For great reading online,
visit www.eHarlequin.com today!

COMING NEXT MONTH

#1609 THE LAWS OF PASSION—Linda Conrad
Dynasties: The Danforths
When attorney Marcus Danforth was falsely arrested, FBI agent
Dana Aldrich rushed to prove his innocence. Brought together by the
laws of the court, they discovered their intense mutual attraction ignited
the laws of passion. Yet Dana wanted more from this sizzling-hot lawyer—
she wanted love....

#1610 CAUGHT IN THE CROSSFIRE—Annette Broadrick
The Crenshaws of Texas
The arousing connection between blue-eyed Jared Crenshaw and
Lindsey Russell was undeniable from the moment they met. Before he
knew it, Jake had woken up in Lindsey's bed, but how had he gotten there?
He was certain they'd been caught in the crossfire of somebody's scandalous
scheme....

#1611 LOST IN SENSATION—Maureen Child
Mantalk
Dr. Sam Holden was still reeling from the past when Tricia Wright swept
him up into a whirlwind of passion. This woman was an intriguing force of
nature: blond, bubbly and hot as hell. But their joint future was put
permanently on hold until he could conquer the past that haunted him.

#1612 DARING THE DYNAMIC SHEIKH—Kristi Gold
The Royal Wager
Princess Raina Kahlil had no desire to marry the man she'd been promised
to. That was until she met Sheikh Dharr Ibn Halim face-to-dashingly-
handsome-face. While Raina found herself newly drawn to her culture and
country, she was even more intensely drawn to its future king....

#1613 VERY PRIVATE DUTY—Rochelle Alers
The Blackstones of Virginia
Federal agent Jeremy Blackstone was the only man Tricia Parker had ever
loved. Now, years after they'd parted, she was nursing him back to health.
Tricia struggled not to fall under Jeremy's sensual spell, but how could she
resist playing the part of both nurse *and* lover?

#1614 BUSINESS OR PLEASURE?—Julie Hogan
Daisy Kincaid quit her job when she realized that her boss, Alex Mackenzie,
would never reciprocate her feelings. But when the sexy CEO pleaded for
her to return and granted her a promotion to tempt her back, would the
new, unexpectedly close business-trip quarters finally turn their business
relationship into the pleasure she desired?

SDCNM0904